"I'm so sorry. I c burned down the whole building."

"But you didn't. It's all right."

Becca shook her head. She was shaking all over. "No. It's not. I—" She began to sniff.

Luke quickly gathered her in his arms. "Oh, don't cry. It *is* all right. Nothing burned down. The only loss is the curtains and mitt, and I'm sure you can replace them without any problem."

His kindness only made her want to cry more, and as much as she enjoyed the comfort of his arms, his nearness was doing nothing to end her trembling. She blinked back the tears and stepped back.

JANET LEE BARTON and her husband, Dan, have recently moved to Oklahoma and feel blessed to have at least one daughter and her family living nearby. Janet loves being able to share her faith and love of the Lord through her writing. She's very happy that the kind of romances the Lord has called her to write can be read by and shared with women of all ages.

Books by Janet Lee Barton

HEARTSONG PRESENTS

HP434—Family Circle
HP532—A Promise Made
HP562—Family Ties
HP623—A Place Called Home
HP644—Making Amends
HP689—Unforgettable
HP710—To Love Again
HP730—With Open Arms
HP745—Family Reunion
HP759—Stirring Up Romance
HP836—A Love for Keeps
HP852—A Love All Her Own

Don't miss out on any of our super romances. Write to us at the following address for information on our newest releases and club information.

Heartsong Presents Readers' Service
PO Box 721
Uhrichsville, OH 44683

Or visit www.heartsongpresents.com

A Love
to Cherish

Janet Lee Barton

Heartsong Presents

To my Lord and Savior for showing me the way,
To my family for encouraging me along the way,
I love you all.

A note from the Author:
I love to hear from my readers! You may correspond with me by writing:

Janet Lee Barton
Author Relations
PO Box 721
Uhrichsville, OH 44683

ISBN 978-1-60260-574-9

A LOVE TO CHERISH

Our mission is to publish and distribute inspirational products offering exceptional value and biblical encouragement to the masses.

PRINTED IN THE U.S.A.

one

Eureka Springs, mid-January 1902

Becca Snow entered the home she'd lived in for most of her life, wondering if she'd live there for the rest of it. She took off her winter coat and hung it on the coatrack, hoping to slip upstairs without being seen.

But the pocket doors separating her sister's dress shop from the rest of the house were open, and her mother had the best hearing in town. "Becca, dear. Come have some tea with us, and tell us about your day," she called.

Becca sighed and forced a smile to her lips as she entered the room and took the cup of tea her mother had already poured for her. Afternoon tea had been a family tradition ever since she could remember. "Good afternoon, Mama, Meagan, and Sarah. My day was fine." It was just a day as all of them had become for her. No problems, but no excitement or joy of doing her job anymore. It seemed she just went from one day to another. "How was your day?"

"Busy but good," her sister Meagan said.

Becca took a tea cake to go along with her tea and sat down in one of the chairs flanking the settee where many of the shop's customers sat and went over her sister's designs or the latest fashion magazines before placing an order.

Meagan had started her dressmaking business sixteen years earlier to help out her family after their father died. She continued with the business even after she married banker Nate Brooks, and she'd made a name for herself in Eureka Springs. The dress shop had thrived, with their mother and sister Sarah coming into the business as well. Becca had helped out in the shop after school and on Saturdays until she went to college, but she'd never wanted to be a seamstress or designer like her sisters. Now, with Meagan's daughters, fourteen-year-old Lydia and twelve-year-old Eleanor, becoming involved in the sewing, Becca was glad she hadn't wanted to go into the business. Not to mention that Sarah, who'd been married to Mitch Overton for two years, had found out she was expecting a few months ago. If the baby was a girl, then she might well want to be part of the business, too.

The shop had made a very good living for them all and provided travel abroad to visit the fashion houses in Paris and even for Becca's education so that she could become what she'd always dreamed of—a teacher. And she would always be thankful. She did love teaching, but it was harder to go about her normal routine now that her dreams had died along with her fiancé.

Becca sipped her tea in silence as conversation flowed around her. She couldn't think of anything to add to it and was hoping that she could escape before her mother or siblings commented on her quietness. No wonder her life was boring—she'd become boring, too.

"Becca? Dear, are you all right? You haven't heard a word we've been saying."

She looked up to see her mother looking at her with concern in her eyes. Her sisters were watching her closely, too. "I'm sorry. I must have been woolgathering." Becca stood and put her cup back on the tray. "I'll take these to the kitchen for you."

"Not now, dear." Her mother took the tray from her. "Please sit back down. We need to talk to you."

"You all look so serious. What did I do?"

"You haven't done anything, Becca. We just worry about you," Sarah said.

That brought tears to Becca's eyes. "I'm sorry."

"Oh, Becca. We're sorry that you've had to go through so much sorrow. We just want to help," Meagan said. "Mama told me that you feel you might do better if you could get away from Eureka Springs."

"I've wished that I could. At least for a while," Becca admitted. "It's not that I want to be away from you all. I would miss you. But. . .it's just so difficult to. . ." She swallowed hard and looked at her sister. "And I don't know—will I ever feel happy again—anywhere?"

Her family quickly gathered around her in a group hug, and that was more than she could take. Becca gave in to the tears she thought she'd used up months ago. Several minutes passed before she had them under control, and once she was down to a sniff or two, her mother poured another cup of tea—her answer for any stressful situation—and brought it to her.

"We have an idea that might help you, dear. We were talking about it earlier today."

"What is it?"

Meagan pulled out a newspaper. "Natalie's aunt Abigail knows you've been struggling and sent this to us. There is an opening for a high school teacher in Hot Springs. Or at least there was a week or so ago."

Becca took the newspaper and scanned the help-wanted ad in the *Sentinel Record*. She tried to tamp down the hope that sprang in her heart. "Do you think the position is still available?"

"I don't know, but I can have Nate find out if you want me to."

Becca looked at her mother and sisters. "I think I need to get away for a while. It's not you all. It's this town and the. . ." She couldn't keep her voice from wobbling, and she hated that she wasn't stronger. She took a deep breath and finished. "The memories."

Her mother hugged her once more. "I will miss you terribly, Becca. But I want you to be happy, to get your joy of life back. If moving to Hot Springs will help, then I want you to go. It's not all that far by train. My goodness—we've been to Europe and back."

"Thank you, Mama," she whispered. "But what about you? I don't want you to live here all alone."

"That's something we were going to tell you at dinner," Sarah said. "With the baby coming, Mitch and I have been talking about buying a home. The small apartment we are in now won't be large enough for long. Mama said we could move in here until we could save enough money to buy something. So we would be here with Mama, and you wouldn't have to worry about her—not that you should anyway. Meagan and I would make sure Mama is all right."

"I know. But still—"

"Girls, I am perfectly able to take care of myself. But Becca dear, Sarah is right. There is no need for you to worry about me. She and Mitch will be here with me."

Becca could hardly believe that she might really get her

wish. She looked at her older sister. "Will you have Nate see what he can find out?"

"I'll get him on it right now." Meagan hurried to the telephone and rang through to the operator. After getting the bank's switchboard, she was connected with her husband. Several minutes of conversation followed before she hung the receiver back on its hook and turned to her family.

"Nate is going to send Marcus Wellington a telegram. He'll get back to us quickly about it."

Becca was almost afraid to hope, but if the position was still open, it seemed this might well be the answer to her prayers. Her stepniece, Natalie, Nate's daughter, came into the shop just then, bringing a couple of beautiful hats she'd designed. Unlike Becca, she'd wanted to go into the fashion business along with the rest of the Snow family, but her true love and talent lay in making lovely hats to go with her stepmother's creations.

Once she found out that Becca was thinking about applying for a teaching position in Hot Springs, she became very enthusiastic. "Oh, Becca! That would be wonderful. I love going to Hot Springs. It's about time I visited my aunt and uncle. If you are there, I'd have even more reason to pay them a visit."

Becca could feel a bud of excitement beginning to open but was afraid to give in to it. What if the position was already taken or she didn't get it? Instead she busied herself with taking the tea tray to the kitchen, setting the table while her sisters helped their mother with dinner, and waiting for Nate to pick up Meagan.

By the time he got there, however, the possibility that she could start a new life away from the memories of Richard and what could have been had her praying that it would be so.

When Nate arrived, Meagan brought him back to the kitchen, and Becca turned from taking the biscuits her mother had made out of the oven.

"I telegraphed Marcus, and he's already gotten back to me. The teaching position is still open, and they haven't had many applications at all. With this being the middle of the school year, there aren't that many people looking for a job. But they need someone soon. One of the married teachers had to resign because she is. . .with child. The principal has been teaching the class, and he's desperate to hire a good teacher."

"You mean there is a possibility that I might get the position?"

"Becca, if you want it, I'm almost certain you will get it," Nate said. "Marcus was going to talk to the principal tonight and said he'd get back to us first thing tomorrow. He and Abigail will give you a high recommendation, I know."

For the first time since Richard had died, Becca felt a flicker of joy. *Dear Lord, please, if it be Your will, let me get this teaching position.*

❧

When Becca got home from work the next day, she learned that Nate had word from Marcus. He'd talked to the principal himself and also to the school superintendent. Going on the Wellingtons' recommendation and desperate to have a teacher, they were quite willing to hire Becca—provided she could be there in two weeks' time.

"I'm not sure I can do that," Becca said. "I can't leave my school in a bind."

"I saw Molly Bryant at the soda shop just the other day.

She is back home and hoping to find a teaching position next year," Sarah said.

"Really?"

"Ring her home and see. If she hasn't found anything yet. . ."

Becca hurried over to the telephone and asked the operator to connect her to the Bryant home. In moments she heard Molly's voice on the other end of the line.

After welcoming her sister's friend home, Becca got right to the point. "Sarah says you want a teaching position next year."

"Yes, I'm hoping to find one," Molly said.

"Would you be willing to start earlier, if possible?"

"I'd love to. But I talked to Superintendent Mallard just the other day, and he said there wasn't anything now."

"Well, there will be once I give them my notice. I'm taking a position in Hot Springs, if the school can find someone to take my place."

"Really?"

Becca smiled at Molly's squeal of excitement and held the receiver away from her ear for a moment. "Really. But I haven't given notice yet. I'll do that first thing tomorrow. May I give your name as a possible replacement?"

"Oh, Becca, yes, please do."

"I will be glad to." Thrilled was more like it. If they allowed Molly to take her place, she could be beginning a new chapter in her life very soon.

"And please thank Sarah for mentioning me."

"I will. Hopefully by this time tomorrow, we'll both have what we want." Becca ended the conversation and turned back to her family with a grin. "I think it's all going to work out."

She prayed that it would. By the time she went to bed that evening, her hopes were high that she could get away from the daily routine that brought back so many painful memories. Each time she passed the police station or the bank or saw Richard's parents at church or in town, memories of him came flooding back. The past year had been so very hard.

She'd made it through one holiday after another—but just barely. She'd managed to get through Thanksgiving by being thankful for the family who had gotten her through the worst of her sorrow. But Christmas had been hard, and now the New Year was here. . .but it loomed long and empty for her without Richard. She didn't know if moving away would help, but she desperately wanted—needed—to find out.

❧

The next afternoon Becca raised her hand to knock on the principal's door and paused to whisper a prayer. "Dear Lord, please let Mr. Johnson see how much I need a change and be open to letting Molly take my place. You know how badly I need to get away."

Her light knock was answered with a "Come in."

She smoothed her skirts and took a deep breath before entering. The secretary was at her desk right outside the principal's inner office.

"Becca, what brings you here this afternoon?" Caroline Green asked.

"I need to speak with Mr. Johnson, if he's not too busy, please."

"I'm sure he'll see you. Wait here, and I'll see." Caroline knocked on the door separating the two offices, and stuck her head in. "Mr. Johnson, Becca Snow would like to speak to you, if you have the time."

"Why of course I do, Miss Green. Send her right in."

Caroline motioned for Becca, who quickly crossed the room and entered the office. "Good afternoon, Mr. Johnson. Thank you for seeing me."

She was aware that Caroline went back to her desk but left the door open, as was the custom when one of the female teachers met with the principal.

"Good afternoon, Miss Snow." He motioned for her to take the chair across from his desk. "What can I do for you?"

Becca sat down and folded her hands in her lap. "Mr. Johnson, I would like to take a teaching position in Hot Springs, and I—"

"Oh no, Miss Snow. We don't want to lose you."

"I'm sorry, sir. It isn't that I don't want to be here. It's just— I feel I must get away from. . ." Becca sighed. "The memories are—"

"It's all right, Miss Snow. I do understand." Mr. Johnson leaned back in his chair. "In fact, I expected something like this after you lost your fiancé. But I was beginning to think that maybe you were through the worst of it all."

"I'm sorry."

"My dear Miss Snow, there is no need to apologize. You've been through a great deal in the last year. You will be able to finish the term, won't you?"

"They would like me to start as soon as possible." She bit her bottom lip, waiting for his reply.

"That does present a problem, doesn't it?"

"Not necessarily. Miss Molly Bryant is back home and looking for a teaching position. She asked Superintendent Mallard about next year a few weeks back, but of course there were no openings at that time."

"Molly Bryant. Yes, I remember her. This means a lot to you, doesn't it, Miss Snow?"

"Yes, sir, it does."

He nodded. "Ask Miss Bryant to come in to see me tomorrow. In the meantime I'm having a meeting this afternoon with Superintendent Mallard and will talk to him about the situation."

Becca jumped up from her chair and would have hugged the man if propriety allowed for it. Instead she simply smiled and said, "Oh thank you, Mr. Johnson. I will speak to Molly as soon as I get home. I'm sure she will come in tomorrow."

"I'll see you tomorrow also. Perhaps we can have this settled by the end of the day. Good day, Miss Snow."

❧

Luke Monroe looked up as his employer entered the office of the building Luke managed when he wasn't off on assignment. Through the years they had become good friends and didn't stand on ceremony. "Marcus! You must have a good assignment lined up for me to show up this early in the day."

Marcus Wellington owned Wellington Agency, the private investigative/protective agency Luke worked for. Marcus spent most of his time in the new office he'd had built farther down on Central Avenue. The office Luke was using had been the first office of the Wellington Agency. Now offices were spread across the state, and Marcus was debating whether or not to expand.

The older man took a seat across from Luke. "It's not exactly an assignment for you. More like a favor to ask."

"You have it. You know that." Marcus couldn't ask anything of him that Luke wouldn't try his best to do. He owed the man his very freedom. After being falsely accused of a crime when he was much younger, Luke had been proven innocent only through Marcus's investigation of the events. Not only had Marcus gotten him out of prison, but he had also taught Luke all he knew about being a private investigator and put him in charge of the building where his office and apartment were located, giving Luke a place to call home. All Luke wanted was to make as much of a difference in someone's life as Marcus had made in his.

"I was wondering if you have a vacant apartment in the building?"

"I do. The Wilsons just moved out. I haven't had time to call anyone on the list, though."

Marcus nodded. "Good. Abigail's niece has an aunt by marriage who has taken a teaching position at Central High School, and while Abby and I are going to invite her to stay with us, I've a feeling she's going to want a place of her own."

"I'll make sure to have it aired out and cleaned, then."

"I'd also just ask you to keep an eye on her. She's never lived totally on her own for any length of time, and she's recently suffered some heartache."

"I understand. I'll be sure to watch out for her. When will she be arriving?"

"I believe Rebecca and our niece Natalie will be here in a week or two. Abby is so excited about it. She can't wait to see Natalie and is hoping to convince her to open a hat shop in town. She'll most likely be spending a lot of time with Rebecca while she's here, and that's another reason I'll feel better about Rebecca living here if she doesn't choose to stay with us. I know you'll watch out for them. They won't have to be watched around the clock, but this is a new town to them and—"

"I understand."

"I knew you would." Marcus stood to leave. "You are a good man, Luke. I always feel better when I put you in charge of something."

Luke was glad he did. But he wasn't so sure he felt the same way this time. It was one thing to investigate people or protect people who came to Hot Springs. But to have the responsibility of keeping someone connected to Marcus's family safe. . .well, that was a big one. He'd do his best though. It was the least he could do after all Marcus had done for him.

two

Almost two weeks later, on the twenty-ninth of January, Becca was on her way to Hot Springs along with her stepniece, Natalie Brooks. She wasn't sure who was more excited—herself because she was moving to a new place and getting away from painful memories, or Natalie because she was getting to show her stepaunt a town she loved.

The trip hadn't been bad at all with Natalie to keep her company. They'd left Eureka Springs the evening before, and Natalie's father had paid extra to get them a private sleeping booth. They'd talked long into the night, like two schoolgirls on their first outing alone. Finally the rocking motion of the train had lulled them both to sleep, and it was only the porter's knock on the door the next morning announcing that breakfast would be served in the dining car in half an hour that stirred them.

They hurriedly helped each other become presentable before joining the other travelers heading to the dining car. Becca knew they both looked nice in the traveling dresses her sister had made them. Meagan had insisted on furnishing her with several new outfits, and the brown and cream dress she had on was one of her favorites.

Becca's appetite had been almost nil since Richard's death, but as the waiter set their breakfasts in front of them, she found that she was suddenly very hungry. It was a welcome change, and after a silent prayer, she took a piping hot biscuit and buttered it.

"Mmm. This is very good."

"Yes, it is," Natalie said. "Traveling always makes me hungrier than usual."

Becca took a sip of steaming coffee and looked out the window. The scenery was a little different from home, but not so much that she felt she was in a strange land, and with Natalie along, she hadn't had a chance to miss her family yet.

The morning sped by as they took their time with breakfast and visiting with other travelers. By the time lunch came around, Becca was filled with anticipation of arriving in Hot Springs. She could barely contain her excitement through the next few hours and was glad she had Natalie with her for company.

They freshened up as best they could and took their seats for the last half hour before their arrival. "I'm so glad you came with me, Natalie."

"I'm just happy you are moving here. I'll miss you so much, but I understand your need to get away. I can at least see you when I come to visit Aunt Abby and Uncle Marcus."

Becca's memories of Natalie's aunt weren't all that good— she'd been awful to Becca's sister Meagan back before Meagan had married Nate. Then Abigail had moved to Hot Springs and married Marcus Wellington. Meagan said that Abigail had changed for the better, but still, Becca was a little nervous that she'd be staying with the couple until she could find an apartment or boardinghouse to live in. At the same time, she was thankful to have a place to stay.

"It's kind of them to invite me to stay with them. I'll begin looking for a place as soon as I can, though."

"There isn't any hurry, Becca. I'm sure you'll be welcome

there as long as you want to stay."

"I won't want to wear out my welcome."

Natalie shook her head and laughed. "You won't. Just wait and see."

Becca could only hope her stepniece was right. The enormity of what she'd done by leaving her teaching position for one in a town she'd never visited and where she really knew no one was beginning to sink in. And yet, so was the relief she felt that she didn't have to pass by daily memories of broken dreams. She'd been praying for guidance and hoped she was doing the Lord's will by moving. And she reminded herself that she wasn't alone. She had Him with her no matter where she went.

As they neared the town that would be her new home, Becca prayed, *Dear Lord, please forgive me for not always remembering that You are always there for me. I know You have been—I couldn't have made it this last year without You. I admit to being nervous about this move. Please give me peace in knowing that You will always be there to guide me, and please help me to do Your will in all that I do. In Jesus' name, I pray. Amen.*

"Look, Becca." Natalie pointed out the window. "Hot Springs is just around the bend up ahead."

Becca held her breath, waiting for a glimpse of the town she'd be claiming as hers soon. The winter scene allowed for seeing the city long before the other seasons would have. Becca's heart began to pound as she saw the first rooftops in the distance. She could make out light spirals of smoke coming from their chimneys, and as the train rounded the bend, the downtown area came into view. She took in everything she could as the train slowed and entered the town set inside Hot Springs National Park.

The valley between two mountains seemed to narrow as the train made its way to the depot. Before the train came to a stop, Becca and Natalie stood and brushed their skirts and pinned on the hats Natalie had made to match their traveling outfits.

As they made their way down the aisle and stepped off the train, Becca felt the peace she'd prayed for and smiled. She might not know anyone here, she might not know her way around, but she would never be alone.

❧

Abigail Wellington stood beside her husband and waited for her niece to alight from the afternoon train. She couldn't wait to see her. She'd loved Natalie as if she were her own since the day she was born, and she didn't see her near often enough, to her way of thinking. Perhaps with her stepaunt, Becca Snow, who was only four years older than Natalie, moving here to take a teaching position, Natalie would come to Hot Springs more often. Abigail hoped so.

In the meantime she hoped she could befriend Becca Snow, the sister of the woman who had married the man she once thought she loved. Abigail felt it was the least she could do to make up for the pain she'd once caused Meagan and Nate. She knew she'd been forgiven years ago, and not a day went by that she didn't count her blessings because of it. But if she could do something to help Meagan's sister feel more comfortable in Hot Springs and help her feel at home, then she wanted to do it.

As if he knew how she felt, Marcus squeezed her hand. "It will all be fine, my love. We'll do all we can to help Becca adjust to being away from her family. And Natalie will be here to help her settle in. By the time Natalie goes back to

Eureka Springs, Becca will feel she's part of our family, too."

"Oh, I hope you are right, Marcus. The poor girl has suffered so much heartache in losing her fiancé. I just can't imagine. . . ." She shook her head. "I hope the move here will help her get over her loss and enable her to look to the future with joy."

"Look, I think I see Natalie—isn't that her just about to step down?"

"It is." Abigail hurried forward. "Natalie! Natalie, dear, over here!"

Her niece spotted her, and Abigail was rewarded with a huge smile. "Aunt Abby!"

Natalie hurried down the steps and ran toward her. Abigail greeted her with a hug and looked over her niece's shoulder to see Becca Snow standing quietly behind her. "Becca?"

At the younger woman's nod, Abigail smiled and gave her a hug also. "Welcome to Hot Springs. We hope you'll love our city as much as we do, don't we, Marcus, dear?"

"We certainly do. Welcome to our town, Miss Snow," Marcus said.

"Oh, please call me Becca, Mr. Wellington. I am looking forward to starting my new position and getting settled in. Thank you both for letting me stay with you until I can find a place of my own. I really appreciate it."

"We're very glad to have you," Abigail tried to assure her. "We can talk more about that at dinner. I'm sure you are both tired. Marcus will take care of getting your things delivered to the house, and we'll get you home so that you can both freshen up before dinner."

Soon they were all in the surrey and on their way back to the house. "You both look lovely," Abigail said. "Natalie, are those hats some of your own creations?"

"They are," Natalie said, nodding. "I made mine and Becca's to match our traveling suits."

"They are beautiful. You are very gifted, Natalie. I'd like you to make one or two hats for me while you're here, if you have time."

"I'd love to do that, Aunt Abby. If you aren't in any hurry, I'm sure I'll have time once Becca begins her teaching position."

Abigail laughed. "No, I'm not in any hurry at all. I want to keep you here as long as possible. You take all the time you need." She glanced over at Becca. "I am very thankful that you are moving here, Becca. I am hoping that Natalie will be visiting more often now that you'll be here."

"Oh, you don't need me to get her here. She was very excited about coming to see you, Mrs. Wellington."

"Please, you must call me Abigail—or Abby, as Natalie does. We want you to feel comfortable around us and know that you can turn to us for any kind of help at any time, Becca."

"Thank you, Mrs.—Abigail. It will be good to know there are people I can turn to if needed."

❧

After a light tea so as not to spoil their dinner later, Becca was shown to a beautiful room across the hall from Natalie's. It was done in blue and white and was quite inviting. It even had a private bath. Her luggage was waiting for her, and Becca was glad for the chance to freshen up and change into a modest dinner dress.

Abigail and her husband were very gracious, and Becca had no doubt they were trying to make her feel comfortable.

Her sister Meagan had assured her that they would be, and it appeared she was right. In the meantime Becca was very thankful that she had a place to stay and that Natalie was with her. Desperate to have her, the school had given her a little more time than they'd originally wanted to. She was to start teaching in less than two weeks, on Monday, the tenth of February, and that didn't give her long to find a place of her own and get moved in. She hoped the Wellingtons would have some recommendations for a nice boardinghouse or apartment building she would feel safe in.

Natalie swept into her room. "Are you ready to go down for dinner? It smells wonderful. I think Aunt Abby had her cook make all of my favorites."

"I'm sure she did. It's obvious that she is thrilled to have you here." Becca pinched her cheeks and checked her hair in the mirror. "I'm ready. I don't want to be late to dinner my first night here."

Natalie led the way downstairs, and Becca was introduced to Marcus's parents, who'd been invited, too. They seemed very nice, and as they went into the dining room, Becca began to relax and think she'd made the right decision to move.

Natalie was right. Her aunt had made sure all of her favorites were served, and the resulting feast reminded Becca of Thanksgiving at home. Everyone seemed quite interested in Becca's new teaching position.

"You are teaching at the high school? How do you like teaching young people, Miss Snow?" the older Mrs. Wellington asked.

"I love teaching, Mrs. Wellington. I've found teaching upperclassmen quite enjoyable."

"The principal, Edward Fuller, is a good friend of ours, and I can tell you that he is more than a little relieved to be able to get back to his work and let you do the teaching." Mr. Wellington chuckled.

"I am just so thankful that you let us know there was a position open. I really needed a change." Becca didn't want to go on about the past. She was sure everyone here knew about Richard's death and—

"We're glad you came here, dear." Mrs. Wellington reached over and patted her shoulder. "I'm certain your students are going to love you—especially after dealing with Edward. He's a wonderful person and a great principal. He's a very good teacher, too, but he readily admits that he is finding it hard to do both jobs."

"I'm sure it is."

"Oh, I think it is probably good for him. Reminds him of what it's like for the teachers," Mr. Wellington said.

Becca smiled and broached the subject uppermost in her mind. "I was wondering if any of you could recommend a nice boardinghouse or apartment building for me to check into."

"My dear, there is no need to hurry. You are welcome here as long as you would like to stay," Abigail said.

"Yes, you are, Becca," Marcus added. "You are more than welcome to stay here. There is no need to worry about finding a place right now."

Becca sensed they were sincere, but she felt it was time she was on her own. She couldn't take advantage of their kindness. "I thank you so much. You are very kind and gracious. But as I plan on making Hot Springs my home, I really believe I need to find a place of my own."

"You young women are getting to be so independent these

days. I don't know whether to be excited or afraid for you," the older Mrs. Wellington commented.

"It's exciting, isn't it?" Natalie said.

"I'm not sure it would be for me, were I your age, dear," Mrs. Wellington stated. "I was taught that a young lady married and took care of the household. But I can see where it would be very exciting for those of you who've had training to do something else—at least for a while. I still hope that you will get married one day."

Not knowing what to say, Becca took a bite of her food, barely tasting it. She knew the older woman didn't mean to bring up hurtful memories, but she suddenly lost her appetite. She'd wanted to be married much more than she wanted to be a teacher, but that wasn't to be after Richard's death.

She hadn't realized that quiet descended after Mrs. Wellington's remark until the woman gasped and said, "Oh my. Becca, I am so sorry, my dear. I didn't mean—"

"It's all right, Mrs. Wellington. I know you didn't. Please don't worry about it."

"I can't believe I was so—"

"Mother Wellington, you are one of the kindest women I've ever known. We all know you meant no harm. But we do want you to know how sorry we are at your loss, Becca," Abigail said. "And while we truly would love for you to stay with us indefinitely, if you feel you would be more comfortable on your own, then we will do our best to help you find a safe place to stay."

"Thank you, Abigail. I do believe that will be for the best. I appreciate your hospitality more than I can say, but I don't want to disrupt your daily lives forever."

"Well, since it is your wish to be on your own, I may have

the answer," Marcus offered.

"Marcus, what do you have in mind?" Abigail asked.

"There is a vacancy in my building downtown. I checked with Luke, and he agreed to hold it just in case Becca chose to be on her own. I haven't mentioned it because I didn't want her to think that we didn't want her here."

"Oh, I love that building," Natalie said. "I used to enjoy going there with you and Uncle Marcus, Aunt Abby. I always thought it would be wonderful to live in one of the apartments there."

"Oh, Marcus, that is a wonderful idea. With Luke right there on the premises, that may be the answer," Abigail said.

"You have an apartment building?" Becca asked.

"Yes. It's right downtown and not that far from the school," Marcus explained. "You can walk or use the trolley to get there. It is where my first office was, and I lived in an apartment there before Abigail and I were married. Luke Monroe manages the building for me now, and I know we'd all feel better knowing you were in that building. I could recommend some boardinghouses, too, but you'd only have a room there, where the apartment would provide you with a home, small though it might be, and I get the feeling that is what you would like."

"That sounds wonderful." Becca really didn't like the idea of living in a boardinghouse—except for having meals provided. She wasn't a very good cook. But she didn't like the idea of being confined to a room all of the time. She could learn to cook. And as large as Hot Springs was, there was sure to be restaurants when she got tired of her own cooking. "Do you think I might be able to see it tomorrow?"

"Of course. I'll telephone Luke after dinner and let him know we'll be coming over after breakfast."

"Thank you all so much. It is wonderful to have you all to turn to." Becca found her appetite had returned. She was starting on a new adventure, and she had to put the past to the back of her mind.

❧

The next morning Luke was on the lookout for the Wellingtons and their houseguest. He'd made sure the apartment was cleaned and aired out just as he'd promised Marcus he would. He'd always liked that each apartment in the building had nice windows and lots of light. This one had the added advantage of looking out onto Central Avenue, just as his did.

Consisting of a nice-sized parlor, a dining room, a small kitchen with its own window, a large bedroom, and a private bath, he thought it would appeal to just about anyone who didn't have children. Some of the apartments in the three-story building had two bedrooms, and a couple of families with one or two children lived in them. Mostly though, single working people who wanted to live close to their work rented the apartments. Only one other lady lived there alone. A widow who worked at the bookstore, she kept pretty much to herself. Maybe if Miss Snow took the apartment, Mrs. Gentry would feel more comfortable.

He wondered what Miss Snow was like. He didn't know many women who were dependent on themselves for their livelihood. Marcus had told him that she'd suffered a heartache of some kind, but Luke didn't feel he should ask for details. He didn't even know how old she was, but if she was Natalie's aunt, she could be Abigail's age. It really didn't matter. He'd promised Marcus he would keep an eye on her, and even if she decided not to take the apartment, he would find a way to watch out for her.

He heard Marcus's voice in the foyer and knew he'd find out soon. He opened the door to welcome them into his office. "Good morning, everyone. It's a beautiful day out, isn't it?"

"Good morning, Luke. It's good to see you," Abigail said. "You remember Natalie, don't you?"

"Of course I do. How are you, Natalie?"

"I'm fine, thank you for asking. I'd like you to meet my aunt. She's my stepmother's sister and my best friend, Becca Snow. Becca, this is Luke Monroe."

Luke had been trying not to stare at the young woman ever since she walked inside his office. She couldn't be more than a few years older than Natalie, and she was quite pretty, with large green eyes and reddish hair. He had a feeling it wasn't going to be a hardship to watch over her.

She smiled at him, showing twin dimples. "Pleased to meet you, Mr. Monroe."

No, watching over Miss Snow wasn't going to be hard at all.

three

"How do you do, Miss Snow? Marcus tells me that you've come to Hot Springs to teach."

"Yes, I have. I'm looking forward to teaching high school very much."

Luke Monroe's smile reached his eyes, and Becca's pulse quickened as he took her hand. "I hope you'll like it here in our fair city."

"I like what I've seen so far," Becca said. Mr. Monroe seemed to be a very nice man, and though his smile warmed her heart, Becca didn't welcome the feeling and hoped the small talk was about to end as she slipped her hand out of his. She really wanted to see her possible new home. Evidently it showed, because Luke went to his desk and retrieved a key.

"I'm sure you are anxious to see the apartment we have available."

"Yes, I am."

Luke motioned to them all to follow him into the elevator that stood ready to take them up. "Marcus just had the elevator put in a couple of years ago, and all of our tenants love it. But there are stairs, too, in case it breaks down or one doesn't want to wait for it."

Becca stepped into the wire cage and enjoyed the ride up to the third floor. She quite liked elevators. Most of the ones in use in Eureka Springs were in hotels and banks, and she didn't have much opportunity to use them. But if she took the apartment, she'd be able to ride it each day.

The elevator stopped long before she was ready for the ride to end, but she was anxious to see the apartment. She hurried off and waited for the Wellingtons, Natalie, and Mr. Monroe to join her in the hall.

As they made their way down the hall, Becca fought the memory of the plans she and Richard had made to build a home. The life she would be living here would be so very different from what she'd hoped for just over a year ago, and she wondered if she'd made a mistake in leaving her family and everything familiar to her, just to get away from the memories. Could she ever really get away from them?

Luke stopped at an apartment that faced the street and turned to her. "I'll unlock the door and show the apartment to you. After that, I'll let you look around all you want."

"Thank you." Becca held her breath while he turned the key. What if she didn't like it? She didn't want to upset the Wellingtons or Natalie.

Luke opened the door, and from the moment she walked inside the small foyer, Becca loved the apartment. The parlor was large and airy with sunlight streaming in from the large bay window. Her spirits lifted immediately. The room was furnished with a nice divan and comfortable chairs. And the bay window was huge. A nice-sized round table and two chairs looked right at home in it. Becca knew she would eat most of her meals right there. She could also see herself sitting there, grading papers and looking out onto the street below, and when it got colder, she'd move to sit near the fireplace to read or work. The room had a cozy feel, and she knew she could think of this place as home, especially after she added the personal touches she'd brought from Eureka Springs—with more to be sent once she had a place of her own.

"It's very nice." She crossed the room to look out of the window. "I like how it looks out over Central Avenue."

Natalie joined her. "Oh look, you can see Bathhouse Row from here. I love the magnolia trees. In the summer they smell so sweet and their blooms are very big."

Becca turned back to Luke. "I'm sorry; let's see the rest of it."

"There is a good-sized dining room to your right—"

"Oh look, Natalie, there are big windows on two sides. I love the light in here." Becca followed Luke into the room, while Natalie, Marcus, and Abigail came in behind her.

A buffet sat along one wall next to a dining table that could easily seat eight. It would be nice to have Natalie and the Wellingtons over for dinner—if she learned to cook well enough. "It's beautiful—it really is."

"Let me show you the kitchen," Luke said. Back in the parlor, he turned to the room next to the dining room. "It's quite functional, I think. The one in my apartment is just like it, and I've found it to be easy to cook in."

The kitchen had a small range, a sink, and a small icebox on one side and a long row of cupboards with a soapstone countertop along the other side. There was even a small window at the end.

"This is the service door," Luke said as he opened another door to the hall. "Coal for the range will always be here, you can put your trash in the receptacle for the janitor to collect, and your grocery deliveries should be left here for easy access."

"I think it will be quite workable. I like it." Becca smiled.

"Now to the bedroom and bath. They are across the way."

Luke motioned to the doorway on the other side of the parlor. "I'll let you take a look and leave you to discuss things in private. I'll be in my office when you are through."

"Thank you," Becca said. "I don't think we'll be too long."

"Take all the time you need," Luke offered. He gave a little salute and turned to leave.

"I think I'll come back down with you, Luke. We'll leave the ladies to it," Marcus quickly added.

Abigail smiled at her husband. "That's a good idea, dear. I'm sure you and Luke have business to discuss, and that way Becca won't feel rushed."

"That's what I was thinking," Marcus said. He chuckled as he and Luke left the apartment.

Abigail's laughter was light and full of joy. "He is such a wonderful man. And he can almost read my mind. I was hoping they would leave us to look over the apartment at our leisure."

She led the way into the bedroom, Becca right behind her. "Oh, how nice and big it is. And another window—I do love lots of light."

The furniture was a matching set of bird's-eye maple, and a comfortable reading chair and table sat in a corner by the window. There was even a closet to put her clothes in.

Becca passed through the door next to it and found a bathroom that would be her very own. She whirled around and smiled at Natalie and Abigail. "It's just wonderful. The furnishings are all so beautiful. I never expected anything so nice."

"You're right. I think it is perfect for you, Becca," Natalie enthused. They slowly made their way back into the parlor, and Natalie turned to her aunt. "I just don't remember these apartments being quite so nice, Aunt Abby. And I didn't realize they were furnished."

"They are very nice, aren't they? Marcus did just have the bathrooms installed earlier this year, and that has made them the nicest apartments in town. Not all of them have furniture, and I confess I had a hand in furnishing this one. The last renter had no furniture, and there were so many things in our attic. I had Luke come and get enough to make it livable."

"Oh, I love it all. You have impeccable taste, Mrs.—ah. . . Abigail."

"Thank you, Becca. I'm glad you like it. But we have more things in the attic—a lot of furniture and decor items that you might be able to use. We'll go up and let you choose what you might like. I just didn't want you to walk into a completely empty apartment."

"I can't imagine changing anything you've picked out." Becca looked around. "Thank you so much." That the apartment was furnished was a blessing. She certainly didn't have the funds to furnish a place this size—and certainly not with the quality of furnishings Abigail had brought to it.

"Are you going to take it, Becca?" Natalie asked.

"I'd be crazy not to, don't you think?"

"Well yes, I do. But the decision isn't mine."

Becca grinned and shook her head. Natalie never had been one to hide her thoughts. From the time they first met when Becca was ten and Natalie was six, they'd been good friends. When Natalie's father married Becca's sister, they'd been thrilled to be family. "Let me take one more look around, and then we can go talk to Mr. Monroe."

The apartment felt like home. Becca couldn't imagine

finding any place that would feel more comfortable. Besides, there weren't that many apartments available. There were some boardinghouses, but at twenty-six, Becca felt she wanted somewhere to call her own. And this just seemed right to her. As she moved through each room once more, she said a silent prayer that she was right and that, if she was wrong, the Lord would let her know—quickly.

❧

Luke wasn't at all surprised when Marcus told him what to tell Becca the rent was. He was giving her a substantial discount. But as he'd done much the same for Luke—even charging him nothing at first, but telling him it was part of his pay—he wasn't going to question him about it.

"Yes, sir."

"We all know that teachers don't make that much money, but she is almost family, and Abigail wants her to stay here. She's hoping that we'll get to see more of Natalie with Becca here."

Luke nodded. "That's a possibility. They seem quite close."

"Becca is four years older, but she's always been there for Natalie, and for that reason alone, Abigail would want to do all she could to help her settle in here. Besides, the town needs good teachers, and I've heard she's a very good one."

Luke wondered at why the knowledge that Becca Snow was four years older than Natalie caught his attention, but it did. That put him at ten years older than her instead of the fourteen that he'd assumed on first meeting her, given that she and Natalie seemed so close. Ten years didn't seem quite so bad—

"Luke. Luke, the ladies are here," Marcus said.

Luke jumped to his feet. "Ladies, please come in. What did

you think, Miss Snow? Will the apartment suit you?"

A smile lit her face just before she said, "Oh yes, it does. I just hope I can afford it."

When Luke named the figure, she seemed speechless. Then she repeated the figure, and he nodded. "Yes, that's right."

Becca looked as if she might cry as she turned to Marcus and Abigail. "I can't let you do that for me. I know how much apartments go for in Eureka Springs, and—"

"Becca, please," Abigail said, "we can well afford to do this, and it is something we very much want to do. You are part of Natalie's family and, as such, part of ours. We'd like to give it to you rent free, but I know you wouldn't allow us to do that."

"But I—"

"Oh, Becca," Natalie interrupted. "Take it. It's perfect. Don't let a little thing like too low a price keep you from living here." Everyone laughed.

"Well, put that way, how can I possibly refuse?" Becca turned to the Wellingtons and spread out her hands. "Thank you. You won't be sorry. I will take very good care of it, as if it were mine, and—"

"It *is* yours, Miss Snow." Luke handed her the key. "Rent is due on the first of each month."

Becca stood, clasping the key close to her chest while Natalie squealed and hugged her. "Let's go take another look and see what else we need from Aunt Abby's attic."

"Natalie! At the price they are charging me, I don't think I need to take anything else from your aunt and uncle."

"Don't be silly. Aunt Abby will come with us."

"Go on," Marcus said to his wife. "You three have a good day. I need to get to my office, and I know Luke has things to do. How about we meet you all back at the house for dinner?"

"That will be wonderful," Abby said. "May I use your phone to call Bea and let her know you'll be joining us, Luke?"

"Certainly. Thank you for the invitation." He certainly wasn't going to turn down a dinner invitation to the Wellingtons any more than Becca Snow was going to turn down the apartment they were offering her. He was beginning to think that looking after Miss Snow might be the most entertaining assignment he'd ever been given. Becca Snow had already brought a feel of springtime to the Wellington Building. She was young and fresh and beautiful.

❧

The rest of the day seemed to fly by after Becca, Natalie, and Abigail left the apartment building. They went to lunch at a new tearoom in town, and the discussion was all about how to make the apartment even more comfortable than it already felt.

While they waited for their lunch orders, Abigail and Natalie helped Becca start a list of what she might need apart from what was already there.

"You'll need curtains at the windows so no one can see in at night," Natalie said.

"And you need bed linens and a few table lamps and tableware," Abigail stated. "I'm sure we can find anything you need in our attic. We'll take a quick look when we get home."

"Mama will be sending some of my personal things from home, and I have a trunk full of things for when Richard and I got married. I'll arrange to have it sent soon."

"Well, I have plenty you can use until your things arrive. I'm so sorry about your loss, dear," Abigail said once more.

"Thank you. It's been hard. But I think moving here will help a lot. I hope so anyway."

"It will help once you start teaching and meet others. You'll meet quite a few people at church on Sunday, and Marcus and I want to give a dinner party to introduce you to some of the people you'll be working with, too."

"Oh, Abigail, you've done so much already. There is no need to do that. But thank you."

"I love giving dinner parties, Becca. Hosting one to make you feel more at home here will be a joy."

Their lunch came just then, a steaming pot of tea and egg salad sandwiches. Abigail poured the tea and changed the subject back to the apartment and the basics of what Becca might need.

"Your utilities are included in the apartment, but you might want to have a telephone installed. There is one down in the lobby, but there isn't much privacy there."

"I'll contact the telephone company this afternoon then."

"Remember that Luke can let them in if you aren't available. In fact, I can have him take care of it for you, if you'd like."

Becca shook her head. "I'm sure there will be a deposit of some kind. I'll go by when we leave here."

By the time they'd finished eating, Becca had a list of all the things she'd need for the apartment, another list of things to do, and Abigail's recommendations on where to get what. There was a grocer not far from the Wellington Building, as well as a pharmacy. Plenty of other shops were within walking distance, too.

Abigail hired a hack to take her home while Becca and Natalie set out on foot to go to the telephone company and see how far it was to the high school from the apartment. Becca could take advantage of trolleys to get her to work if the walk was too far or the weather was bad.

It didn't take long to arrange for the phone company to install a phone the next week, and after finding the high school, Becca thought she'd enjoy the walk on a good day. She and Natalie took a trolley back to Abigail's home, and Becca found she liked this town more each day. She couldn't wait to get all moved in and begin teaching again.

By the time they arrived back home, they only had time for a quick look at what was in Abigail's attic before it would be time to dress for dinner—but it was enough to know that there was plenty up there to furnish several apartments.

"I almost wish I was moving here, too, Becca," Natalie said as she moved around the furniture, lamps, boxes of whatnots, and any number of other things from her aunt's former homes.

"You could, you know." Becca picked up a lamp she thought would look wonderful in her new bedroom for a closer look. "Wouldn't it be fun to have apartments in the same building? You could open a hat shop here. I'm sure it would do very well."

"It's a thought. Maybe I'll talk to Aunt Abby and Uncle Marcus about the possibilities and where the best location might be. And maybe I'll get up enough nerve to ask Papa what he thinks." Natalie sighed and shook her head. "Somehow, I don't believe he'll be as excited about the prospect of my moving away as I am."

"Probably not. But it would be so nice to have you here." Becca set the beautiful lamp back down carefully.

"I know. I'm going to miss you when I go back home. But I

think you made the right decision for you. I think getting out of Eureka Springs will be good for you and—"

"Natalie, dear, are you up here?"

"Yes, Aunt Abby. Is it time to get ready for dinner?"

"It is." Abigail stepped inside the huge attic. "As you've seen, I have more than enough for you to choose from, Becca. We'll come up in the morning when there is better light. But dinner will be ready in less than an hour, and Marcus and Luke should be here anytime now."

As they headed down to the second floor, Becca realized she was looking forward to many things for the first time in a very long time.

She and Natalie hurried to change into something more fitting than their day dresses for dinner. She was sure that she wouldn't dress for dinner in her own place. She would eat a simple supper and most likely wear what she'd worn to work that day. But she was at the Wellingtons, and they dressed for dinner each night. Becca knew that was what wealthy people did. They changed clothes for most any activity during the day. She did when really necessary, but she didn't see the need in having a new outfit on every time she left the house.

Only because her sister was such an excellent seamstress, Becca had a wardrobe befitting of someone much wealthier than she was, and never had she appreciated it so much as now. Tonight she chose a dinner gown of green silk. It was one of her best colors, and she'd been told it made her eyes darker and brought out the red in her hair.

Natalie knocked on the door just as Becca was finishing her toilette, and they went down the stairs together. It appeared that Marcus and Luke were waiting for them when they entered the parlor, for Abigail whisked them all into the dining room.

It wasn't until Becca was seated next to Luke Monroe that she realized how much she'd been looking forward to seeing him again.

four

By Wednesday of the next week Becca still couldn't believe the apartment was hers. The weekend had passed quickly: She and Natalie and Abigail had rummaged in the attic on Saturday afternoon, and on Sunday she'd gone to church with them all and been welcomed by so many people she couldn't begin to remember all of their names. But Abigail had invited several people back for Sunday dinner, and Becca had met the principal she'd be working for. Mr. Fuller and his wife were so nice she found she was quite excited about starting to work and anxious to get settled in her apartment.

Despite her objections, the Wellingtons were charging her only half a month's rent for February, saying they wanted her to have plenty of time to move and get settled in comfortably. They insisted that she stay with them until the telephone was installed and she had moved all she might need over to the apartment. She'd begun to move in on the first, the day after she rented it, bringing in a few things from the Wellingtons' attic each day after. She was expecting a crate to arrive anytime with the things her mother was sending. She'd see what she needed after that. Abigail had told her that she was welcome to take anything else she needed, but they'd done so much for her already that she didn't want to take more.

The apartment had begun to feel like home. They'd found curtains to hang at the windows and lamps for the parlor and bedroom. Abigail had several sets of tableware in the attic, too, and had told Becca to choose a set she liked. But Abigail's china—even that in the attic—was very expensive, and Becca didn't feel right asking for it. Finally Abigail insisted she take a set of genuine Haviland china that had been made in Limoges, France. It was beautiful, heavily embossed and traced with gold, its design one of sprays of pink roses.

Becca had tried to refuse, but even Natalie had insisted she take the set, and now her cousin was busy unpacking the delicate pieces and handing them to Becca to put in the sideboard in the dining room.

"I can't wait to come to dinner here, Becca. What fun it will be to see your table all set with china and—"

"I've got to learn to cook first, Natalie," Becca replied.

"You can cook. I've seen you in your mother's kitchen."

"You've seen me helping Mama. She did show me how to make some things when Richard and I became engaged." Becca swallowed hard and blinked at the sudden tears that formed.

"I'm sorry, Becca. I didn't mean to bring up hurtful memories." Natalie patted her on the shoulder.

Becca sighed. "It's all right. I was just going to say that I hadn't kept up the lessons afterward. I'm just hoping I can remember what she did manage to teach me."

A knock on the door was a welcome interruption for Becca, and she hurried to the foyer. Thinking it was probably Abigail, she was surprised to see Luke Monroe standing there, a large box propped up on his shoulder. The beat of her heart sped up as it usually did when he smiled at her.

"Good morning, Miss Snow. You've had a trunk and several boxes delivered just now. I wanted to make sure you were here before I brought them up."

Becca backed up and made room for him to come in. "Please just put it down anywhere, Mr. Monroe. I should have let you know to expect them. I'll come help you bring them up."

"No. They are too heavy for you. I'll get them. Just tell me where you want the trunk, and I'll bring it up next." He smiled once more, but Becca could tell from the tone in his voice that he meant what he said.

"If you could put it in the bedroom, at the end of my bed, that would be nice."

"Certainly. And the other boxes?"

"Just put them here in the foyer. And thank you, Mr. Monroe."

"You are quite welcome. It is no problem whatsoever."

"Luke! How are you today?" Natalie came out of the kitchen. "What do you think of the apartment? It is looking quite homey, don't you think?"

For a moment Becca felt a twinge of jealousy that the younger woman knew Luke well enough to call him by his first name, and then she became unsettled that it mattered to her. After all, he was the manager of her apartment building—not a lifelong friend. No. Friends didn't make one feel quite the way Luke Monroe's smile made her feel—all fluttery and nervous.

Luke looked around the room and nodded. "It does look quite comfortable. Makes me feel mine could use a little sprucing up."

Natalie laughed. "Yours probably just needs a woman's touch. When are you ever going to get married, Luke?"

"Natalie!"

"It's all right, Becca. I've been after Luke to find a wife for several years. He's quite used to my impertinence. But I'm afraid he's never going to take my advice."

Luke laughed and shook his head. "I'll bring the trunk up shortly."

"Thank you. I'll leave the door unlocked."

When he left, Becca turned to Natalie. "I can't believe you talked to him that way, Natalie. Why, it was quite—"

"Honest. He does need to get married. He would make someone a wonderful husband."

"Have you set your sights on him, Natalie?"

Natalie's giggle quickly turned to full-blown laughter. "No. Luke is like an uncle to me. I've known him since I was six or seven, Becca. I could never think of him that way. But I do care about him and would like to see him happily married one day. Besides, he's fourteen years older than I am."

"Lots of women are married to men older than them."

"Yes, well, fourteen years seems a bit much to me. Ten wouldn't be so bad, though." She grinned. "No, ten wouldn't be bad at all. In fact, I think that would be just about right."

Becca realized where her friend was going with her thoughts. "Don't even think about it. Not for one moment, Natalie. I'm not looking for romance. I just want to get over heartache."

The younger woman patted her on the shoulder. "Oh I know. And that takes time. But it doesn't appear that Luke is looking, either. And who knows what could happen?"

Becca was long used to her stepniece's romantic notions, and she knew the best way to handle them was to pretend she didn't understand what Natalie was hinting at. So she just sighed and went back to the kitchen—and tried not to think of what could happen. . . .

ॐ

Later that day Becca went to the grocer down the street to stock her kitchen. Abigail had told her that Morton's Grocery Store carried a fine variety of goods.

She chose things she knew she could cook fairly easily. Bacon and eggs along with a loaf of bread would work for several meals. She bought staples like flour, sugar, coffee, and tea. She picked up some canned vegetables and some potatoes, thinking she'd like some fried with onions as she'd seen her mother do. It sounded good for supper. By the time she'd selected other items, Becca felt she could survive several days on her own cooking. She'd spotted several nearby cafés where she could go if she got tired of the few things she knew how to cook.

After arranging for her groceries to be delivered, Becca stepped out of the grocer's, her mind on getting back to the apartment before the delivery boy got there. She turned to the left and collided with a man on his way in. He brushed her to the side and attempted to move.

"Oh, I am so sorry," she said a bit breathlessly as she steadied herself. "I wasn't watching what I was doing."

"Should watch more closely," the man muttered, his eyes boring into hers for one brief moment before he tipped his hat down over his eyes and entered the store without acknowledging her apology. Well, she tried. Something about the man looked familiar to her, but she was sure she'd never met him before. Maybe he had relatives in Eureka Springs.

She shrugged and hurried on her way, excited to be spending her very first night in her apartment. With her things from home unpacked and put up, it really felt like home. It would be the first time she'd ever stayed by herself—Natalie had offered to stay with her, but she'd turned her down. She needed to get used to being alone, and she was actually looking forward to it.

She took the elevator up with Mrs. Gentry, whom she'd just met that morning.

"Good afternoon, dear. Did you get everything unpacked?"

"I did. I've just ordered groceries to be delivered, and I'm staying in the apartment tonight."

"Well, I hope you like it here. It's a very safe building— Luke sees to that—and you'll feel quite safe here after a while."

"Oh, I already do." And she did. She'd met several more of her neighbors besides Mrs. Gentry, and Luke Monroe was just down the hall. She had nothing to fear in this new home—nothing at all.

●

Harland Burrows looked back to see what direction the young woman who slammed into him went. He'd seen that young woman before—he was sure of it—but he couldn't remember just where. He'd lived in Hot Springs for several years now, and it was possible he'd run into her. Still, she was very attractive, and he was sure he would have remembered meeting her. But from the way the hair had stood up on the back of his neck when her eyes met his, he didn't think it had been a good meeting.

"Harland, good day to you. That caviar you ordered came in just this morning," Ned Morton, the grocer, said.

"Hello, Ned. It is a fine day out. I need to add a few more things to the order." He handed the man his list. "It's not a lot, so I can take it with me."

Ned looked over the list and handed it to one of his clerks to fill. "This won't take long."

"Say, that young woman who just left here—I'm sure I know her, but I've forgotten her name. Can you tell me what it is?"

"The pretty one who just left?"

Harland nodded. "Yes, that's the one. I just can't place her."

"First time she's been in here." Ned pulled out a sheet of paper. "She paid cash, so I don't have a name. Just that she lives in apartment 312 in the Wellington Building."

"Well, perhaps it will come to me. If she's new in town, maybe she just looks like someone I know. I'll think on it." He waited for Ned to fill his order, but he couldn't get the woman out of his mind. He'd seen her somewhere before. In his line of business, he depended on remembering the people he'd run into. He had to.

❧

Luke Monroe made it his business to know as much as he could about the people who lived in his building, and as much as possible, he kept up with what was happening in their lives and how they were doing. Most of them had come to feel like family to him.

But there was something different about Becca Snow—a feeling he had each time he saw her that had nothing to do with how he felt about the other renters in the building. And it had nothing to do with the fact that Marcus had asked him to watch over her. It was all about the way his chest tightened when he was around her and how his heart beat faster when she smiled at him. He looked forward to seeing her each day.

When he'd taken her trunk and several boxes up earlier, he was impressed by the warmth and coziness of the apartment. She was making it hers in a way that told him she was someone to whom home and family meant a great deal. What he assumed were family pictures were set here and there, with several hung on the wall. The place had an inviting feeling that made him want to linger. But Miss Snow and Natalie were still busy unpacking and he had work to do, so he'd gone back to his office, only to find himself thinking of how pretty she'd looked as she thanked him for his help and saw him out the door.

There was no way around the fact that she was on his mind quite often. Having her, Natalie, and Abigail in and out of the building while she was moving in had him listening for the lilt of Becca's voice or the sound of her laughter. Still, he told himself that he didn't need to get too interested in the young woman—Marcus knew about his background, and while he trusted Luke to watch out for her, Luke wasn't sure he'd ever approve of him courting Becca. And even if the Wellingtons had no objections, that didn't mean Becca's family wouldn't. In fact, Luke was sure that they would, and he needed to remember it. It was the main reason he'd been able to keep from giving his heart to anyone. There weren't many people who would want a man who'd spent time in prison for a son-in-law—even if he had been cleared of all charges.

But as he watched Becca enter the lobby and head to the elevator, he knew it wasn't going to be easy to stop thinking about her. When she saw him and smiled, he thought it was going to be near impossible.

five

It was getting dark by the time Becca put away all her groceries and thought about what she wanted for her supper. She still had boxes to unpack—books from home and some personal items—so she decided to scramble some eggs and make toast.

Becca loved her kitchen, and she liked that there was a window at the end of it. She opened it just a bit for fresh air, and she could see out to where streetlights were coming on down below. Seeing several lights at windows across the way made her feel safe and not so alone.

Deciding to fry some bacon so she would have grease to cook her eggs in, Becca slipped several pieces in the skillet and set it over the burner. She'd always been a little afraid of stoking the fire in a stove and had depended on her mother to do it. But she managed, and minutes later she was proud that she had cooked the bacon without burning it too badly. It was just nice and crispy. Then Becca put slices of bread into the oven and began scrambling her eggs. The eggs were just the way she liked them when she slid them onto a plate alongside her bacon.

But when she turned to retrieve her toast, black smoke was seeping out of the oven. She quickly grabbed a mitt and pulled the pan out, but the toast was black and the pan was hot. She dropped it alongside the skillet, and the mitt caught on fire. "Oh no!"

Becca hurried to the window and raised it higher, but before she could throw the mitt out the window, the curtain caught on fire. Suddenly Luke burst into the kitchen, and she could only watch as he grabbed the curtains and the mitt, dumped them into the sink, and pumped water on them. The grease in the skillet suddenly flamed up, and Becca felt frozen to the spot as she watched Luke grab the lid and slam it on top of the skillet, quickly smothering the flame.

Only then did she let go of the breath she'd been holding. She began to tremble as she looked at Luke. "Thank you. I—I'm sorry. . .I'm so sorry. I could have burned down the whole building."

"But you didn't. It's all right."

Becca shook her head. She was shaking all over. "No. It's not. I—" She began to sniff.

Luke quickly gathered her in his arms. "Oh, don't cry. It *is* all right. Nothing burned down. The only loss is the curtains and mitt, and I'm sure you can replace them without any problem."

His kindness only made her want to cry more, and as much as she enjoyed the comfort of his arms, his nearness was doing nothing to end her trembling. She blinked back the tears and stepped back. He immediately dropped his arms to his sides.

"I don't know why I thought I could do this. I should have paid more attention to Mama's teaching. I don't know how to cook."

"No? Those eggs look just fine, but they are probably a little cold by now. And the bacon is crisp, just the way I like it." He lifted a piece and took a bite. "Just right. But it's kind of smoky in here. Let's raise some windows, and I'll take you out to eat. I was coming to see if you might like to celebrate moving in, anyway."

"Your timing couldn't have been better. I don't know what I would have done if you hadn't shown up. Now the Wellingtons are going to ask me to move, and I can't blame them. I—"

"Miss Snow, I'm glad I showed up, too. But there's no need to worry about the Wellingtons. I'll not be running to them with any tales. All is well. Let's go eat, and by the time we get back, hopefully there'll not even be a smoky smell. Gather your jacket, and I'll raise the windows."

Becca was so grateful that he wouldn't be telling Marcus and Abigail that she'd nearly burned the place down that she didn't even argue with him. She headed for her room to freshen up and grab her reticule.

"You might want to raise the windows in there, too," Luke called from the dining room. "It might be chilly when we get back, but I'll show you how to turn up the radiator when we return."

Becca did as he suggested, and in a matter of minutes they were seated at a restaurant just around the corner from the building. She had to admit that sharing a meal with Luke Monroe held a lot more appeal than eating cold bacon and eggs.

More than once on the way to the restaurant, Luke told himself he shouldn't have invited Becca Snow to dinner, and now that he was sitting across from her, he knew he was right. Still, he was glad that he had. They'd been shown to a table for two in an alcove that looked out onto the street.

It was nice to have company for the meal. Had he planned to cook for himself tonight, most likely he would have chosen the same menu she had, only he liked making an omelet and fried potatoes to go along with it. But more often than not, he chose to eat out as opposed to eating at home alone. Somehow, seeing other people doing the same thing made him feel less lonely.

"What do you recommend?" Becca asked.

"Everything on the menu is good, but I like the roast beef special."

"I'll have that then."

The waiter came to take their order, and Luke requested the special for both himself and Becca. When the man left, Luke turned to Becca and found her gaze on him.

"Thank you again, Mr. Monroe. I really didn't know what to do when the curtains caught on fire. How did you get there so fast? And what alerted you to the fire?"

"Actually I'd come to see if you needed anything. I wanted to show you how to work the heat, and I did want to invite you to dinner, too. I smelled something on fire, and. . .I just happened to time it right."

"You certainly did. I can't bear to think of what might have happened had you not shown up when you did."

Neither could he. To think that she might have been badly burned. . .or worse. No. He wouldn't let himself think about it. "I'm thankful that I was there. Let's not think about what might have happened and be thankful that it didn't. Will you pray with me?"

"Yes, please pray," Becca said and bowed her head.

Luke looked at her bowed head for a moment before bowing his own head. "Dear Lord, we thank You that Miss Snow was not hurt earlier tonight. We thank You that nothing was burned that cannot be replaced. Please be with Miss Snow as she starts her new teaching position and help her to settle into her apartment and feel at home here in Hot Springs.

Thank You for bringing her here. We thank You for the food we are about to eat. Most of all, we thank You for Your plan for our salvation. In Jesus' name. Amen."

"Amen," he heard Becca whisper from across the table.

"Are you excited about starting work next week?"

"I am. Thank you for praying about it. I can barely wait to meet my students and get to know them. I've met Mr. Fuller, and I'm anxious to meet the other teachers, also."

Their meals arrived just then, and conversation stopped until the waiter left the table. Then Luke waited to see if Becca liked her meal.

"You were right. This is very good."

"I'm glad you like it. Back to our conversation. . .I'm sure everything will go quite well at your new school. I'm sure everyone is anxious to meet you, too. What made you want to be a teacher?"

"I loved playing school with Natalie. I was always the teacher, and she was the student. But I didn't plan to be a real teacher—I thought I would become a seamstress like my sisters and mother."

"Why didn't you?"

Becca chuckled and shook her head. "I found I hated sewing. It was much too solitary for me. And I had the hardest time threading the needle. Besides, there was really no need for another seamstress in the family. The business didn't need that many of us. But I will always be thankful to my sister's business, for it provided me the education to become a teacher."

"Then this isn't the first time you've lived away from home, is it?"

"Oh no. It's the first time I've been on my own or lived

by myself. I went to the Industrial Institute and College in Mississippi along with one of my friends who had family there, but of course I lived in a dormitory with other students, so I was never alone."

"Are you nervous about spending your first night alone?"

"No." She shook her head, and Luke decided he liked the way the light caught the reddish highlights in her hair.

"Good."

"I might be nervous if I weren't in an apartment building. But there are others all around, and everyone seems very nice."

"They are. You'll find that the tenants watch out for each other, and I make sure the building is safe. We have a guard day and night, and they make certain it is safe as well."

"That is good to know. I should have asked more questions before I moved in, I suppose, but the apartment felt so homey to me that I felt safe from the moment I walked in. As it turned out today, the building was safer before I moved in. It wouldn't surprise me if the other tenants don't ask me to leave."

Luke had to laugh with her. It was refreshing to find a woman who could laugh at herself. "The tenants aren't going to know you caught anything on fire. And it's not the first time an apartment has had smoke billowing from under the door. Mrs. Gentry burned some cookies a few weeks back. It happens."

"Well, I'm afraid it might happen more if I don't learn to cook soon."

"You really don't know how?"

"Well, I can cook a few things. But. . ." She shook her head. "Not many. Mama did try to teach me, but I'd like to learn more. I guess it just comes with doing it. She suggested that I find a copy of Fannie Farmer's *Boston Cooking-School Cook Book* and told me that it would teach me all I need to know. I hope she's right."

Luke was tempted to tell her he could teach her, but he stopped himself from doing so. That would mean spending more time with her, and he had a feeling that was something he should try not to do. She was much too captivating for his own good.

❧

When they arrived back at the apartment, Becca was relieved that it no longer smelled like smoke. Luke helped her close the windows and showed her how to manage the heat and light the fireplace. "It should be toasty in here before long."

Becca followed him to the door. "Thank you for putting out the fire, for the meal, and for everything."

"You are quite welcome. Thank you for joining me for dinner. I don't much like eating alone."

"It was nice to have company."

"Good night. Lock up good."

"I will. Good night."

Becca saw him out and made sure to lock up behind him. It had been a very pleasant evening. She had almost forgotten how nice it was to go to dinner with a gentleman. And Luke was certainly that—and a handsome one, too. Surprised at that thought, Becca hurried into the kitchen to clean up the mess she'd left behind.

She hadn't thought of a man that way since Richard, and she wasn't comfortable thinking that way about another man now. Still, she had to fight to keep thoughts of Luke at bay, and she was glad when her telephone rang. It was Natalie, wondering how everything was going.

"Everything is fine. I'm cleaning up the kitchen now, and I'm going to take a nice bath after that."

"It sounds as if you've settled in quite well," Natalie said. "I am almost envious of you. Especially since I've decided to go home."

"You are going back so soon?"

"Well, I have an ulterior motive. I'm going to try to talk Papa and Mama into letting me open a hat shop here. I think it's time I was on my own, too. And I'm going to miss you so, Becca."

"What do you think your parents will say?"

She could hear Natalie's deep sigh over the telephone wire. "I don't know. But I want to try."

"You know you can move in with me, if you need to."

"Of course I know you would welcome me in. But I want to be on my own, just like you are. I think it is time. After all, this is the twentieth century. And I have no suitor in sight. It's time I take on the responsibility of making my own living."

"Oh, Natalie, I'm not sure your papa will agree with you. Remember, my papa died when I was young. Our situations are different."

"Don't you want me to move here?"

"Of course I do. I just don't want you to be disappointed if—"

"I know. And I'll try not to be. But say a prayer that Papa will listen to me at least."

"I will. When are you leaving?"

"Tomorrow afternoon. Aunt Abby wanted me to ask you to lunch."

"Of course I'll come to lunch. Tell her "thank you." Your

aunt and uncle have been wonderful to me, Natalie. I will be forever grateful to them."

"Come about noon. I'd better go pack. I want to get home and get back here as soon as possible. Seeing you start all over here makes me want to do something new. I feel I'm going to become a spinster if I stay in Eureka Springs."

Becca had to keep herself from saying that she would most likely be the spinster of the two of them—not Natalie. After all, she was four years older, and her plans for marriage had died with Richard. But somehow she didn't think those were the words Natalie wanted to hear. Instead she said, "I'll be praying they agree to let you come here, Natalie. For your sake and mine, I'd love to have you nearby."

"That's what I wanted to hear. See you tomorrow."

"See you then." Becca replaced the receiver and went back to the kitchen. It would be nice to have Natalie in the same town. She was going to like it here. She was sure she was going to like her new school, and she loved her apartment. And it didn't hurt at all that Luke Monroe managed the building.

Her thoughts turned to the man who'd saved her from catching the apartment—not to mention herself—on fire. Her heart thudded at the memory of how afraid she had been when the curtains caught on fire. When Luke had suddenly showed up and saved her and the building, she'd felt as if the Lord had surely brought him at just that time and for that reason.

Standing there in the kitchen with her memories, Becca couldn't help but think of how it felt when Luke had held her for that brief moment or two when she'd nearly given in to tears. She'd felt safe and comforted, and it hadn't been easy to step out of the circle of his arms. It hadn't been easy at all. But at the same time, she felt guilty that she'd enjoyed being held by Luke when, just over a year ago, she'd been engaged to marry Richard.

But Richard was gone, and nothing was going to bring him back. Was she to live the rest of her life alone and lonely? That was something she didn't want to think about. Not now, at any rate. Right now she wanted to go take a bath in her very own tub and go to sleep in the first place she could call her own.

Becca gathered her robe and nightgown and went into the bathroom. She almost pinched herself to make sure she wasn't dreaming. Marcus and Abigail had spared no expense when they'd remodeled and had the bathrooms put in. She'd only hoped for an indoor toilet and a basin, expecting to have a communal tub down the hall somewhere, but to have her own tub, well, she felt as if she were living in pure luxury.

She turned on the water and added some bath salts to it. She wasn't going to think about the past tonight. And she wasn't going to worry about the future. She was going to soak in her very own tub and thank the Lord above for her blessings.

⁂

Luke had a hard time going to sleep. All he could think about was Becca Snow. She was so pretty and so very real. She didn't put on airs and gush like a lot of the women he knew. She seemed to be comfortable with who she was, and it was refreshing to be around her.

When he'd come down the hall to see if she needed anything, he'd noticed the smell of smoke right away. But it wasn't until he got close to her door that it seemed the smell and smoky air was coming from her apartment. When he'd heard her yell, "Oh no!" he hadn't waited to knock. He'd grabbed his master key and let himself in.

When he'd run into the kitchen to see flames grab the curtains and Becca standing so close to them, his heart had stopped. He could remember asking the Lord for help, and then he went into action. There was not one doubt in his mind that his prayer had been answered. He'd been able to put the curtains out before they caught anything else on fire and put out the skillet fire before it had a chance to do damage. But it'd been such a close brush with disaster; he knew it would be a long time before he forgot it.

That Becca had held herself together when he was pretty sure all she wanted to do was dissolve into tears said a lot about her character. He'd followed his first instinct when he'd seen the sheen of tears in her eyes and tried to comfort her. That had been his first mistake. When she'd moved away, his arms had felt empty, and he knew he'd remember the moment for a very long time. The second mistake had been in asking her to dinner, but he knew he'd do it again in a minute. He couldn't remember enjoying an evening more.

Still, he reminded himself that he had to quit thinking of her—at least in the way that he was. This was not a woman he could ever hope to court and not one he could ever hope to marry. But somehow none of that mattered when it came to thinking about Becca Snow. He simply couldn't seem to put her out of his mind.

six

On Sunday morning as Becca got dressed for church, she felt totally at home in the apartment and was excited about beginning her new position the next day. The last few days had been busy. She'd had lunch with Natalie and Abigail, and she'd gone to the depot with the Wellingtons to see Natalie off on Thursday. As they'd waved good-bye until the train rounded a bend and couldn't be seen any longer, Becca didn't know who had hated to see Natalie leave worse, her or Abigail.

The older woman had linked her arm with Becca's and said, "I'm going to miss Natalie so, and I know you are, too. You know Marcus and I were never able to have children, and I've always thought of Natalie as more than a niece."

"I know. Hopefully she'll get to come back soon."

"That is what I'm praying for. But I don't want you to become a stranger. Please. Marcus and I enjoy having you around, and we'd love to have you think of our home as yours on Sundays. We have several people over after church for Sunday dinner each week. His parents used to do it, but we've sort of taken that over from them in the last few years. It was becoming too hard for Mother Wellington."

"Thank you, Abigail. I would love to join you for Sunday dinner. Thank you for the invitation."

Becca had kept busy on Friday and Saturday, getting more settled in and buying new curtains for the kitchen. When she'd asked Luke for a ladder so that she could put them up, he'd put them up himself.

He'd asked about her plans for the weekend, and she'd told him that she was going to the Wellingtons for dinner after church. He'd immediately asked if he could escort her since he was always invited for Sunday dinner, too. "It's the one day of the week I never have to decide whether to cook for myself or go out somewhere. I love it. Since we're both going to the same place, we might as well go together."

Although Becca wasn't sure why her heartbeat sped up at his suggestion, it made perfect sense to her, and she saw no reason not to agree. "I suppose we might as well. I can meet you in the lobby—what time do we need to leave?"

"We'll catch the trolley and need to leave about nine."

"I'll be on time."

Now as she dressed in a blue and cream Sunday dress, one of the many new ones Meagan had insisted she needed, Becca was grateful for many reasons. She was grateful for the invitations from both Abigail and Luke, and she was grateful to her sister for providing her with a fashionable wardrobe. It occurred to her that she'd never had to worry about whether she had the latest styles or not. She'd always had them because her sister and mother had a knack for knowing what they would be even before they made it to Eureka Springs.

She left her apartment for the elevator to take her down to the lobby, and a few moments later as she stepped out of the elevator and looked at the clock in the lobby, Becca was relieved to see that she was a few minutes early. She hated to be late when someone was expecting her.

Luke was waiting for her, and he smiled as she approached him. "Good morning, Miss Snow."

"Good morning. I hope I haven't kept you waiting."

"No, not at all. But I will say I'm surprised at your promptness."

"Oh? Why is that?"

He smiled down at her. "Most women I know think it's fashionable to keep a gentleman waiting."

"Oh. Well, I suppose I could learn to do that, but I was taught to be on time if at all possible."

"Then you were taught well, and I appreciate it. We'll have no problem at all catching the trolley. Thinking you would be a little late, I gave you an earlier time than needed. In fact, we'll have to wait a few minutes for it to get here. I apologize. Next week you can wait until a quarter after nine, if you'd like."

Luke truly looked apologetic, and Becca found herself wanting to make him feel better. "No need to apologize. It's all right. But I'll take the extra minutes next Sunday."

Realizing that he was planning on accompanying her to church again next week gave Becca a good feeling deep inside. And after his coming to her aid the night of the fire and promising not to tell anyone how close she'd come to burning the building down, putting curtains up for her, and offering to accompany her to church, she had no doubt that she had made a new friend. One she could count on.

ta

There was no way Luke couldn't enjoy the interested looks he and Becca got as he led her to the pew he normally sat in. It was right behind Marcus and Abigail, and he'd been sitting there for the last ten years. But he'd never sat there with a woman he'd brought to church. He motioned for Becca to enter first and then took a seat beside her. He could hear the twitter of whispers behind them.

Becca had sat with Natalie and the Wellingtons the Sunday before, and he was sure she'd been noticed. He certainly hadn't been able to concentrate on the sermon that day. But today she was sitting beside him, and he was enjoying knowing that many of his church family were more than a little curious about how that came to be. When he'd first begun going to church there, several of the older women had tried their hand at matchmaking, but nothing had developed. He was pretty sure that they'd given up on him long ago.

And truly, Becca sitting beside him changed none of that, but he wasn't going to deny that he very much liked the fact that she was sharing a hymnal with him—even though all they ever would or could be was friends. It seemed he had to keep reminding himself of that fact.

He forced himself to listen to the sermon, and as usual, it was very good. The minister, John Martin, spoke about Ecclesiastes 3:4 and about there being "a time to weep, and a time to laugh; a time to mourn, and a time to dance." He couldn't help but notice that Becca was listening intently.

Marcus had told him that Becca had suffered a heartache but not exactly what. Luke hoped that what she was hearing would help her through whatever had caused her grief, and he prayed her heart would heal.

By the time he and Becca left the Wellingtons' that evening to go back to the apartment building, he couldn't remember spending a more enjoyable Sunday. The meal had been wonderful, as always. They'd played parlor games afterward and had a light supper before he and Becca left. The day in itself wasn't that much different from many he'd spent at the Wellingtons'. What had made it so memorable and enjoyable was Becca's company. She truly was delightful to be around.

"I had such a good time," Becca commented as they walked to the trolley stop near the Wellingtons'. "Thank you for escorting me home, Mr. Monroe."

"You are welcome. But since we see so much of each other, do you think you might just call me Luke? Calling me Mr. Monroe makes me feel old."

"Old? Why, you aren't old. But if calling you by your last name makes you feel that way, of course I can call you Luke. Only if you call me Becca, though."

"I can do that." He'd been thinking of her as Becca for days now. "Becca it is, then."

The trolley stopped, and he held Becca's arm to steady her as she ascended the steps. He followed her to an empty seat and sat down beside her. He was quite a bit older than Becca—ten years by his best estimation. Just one more reason to keep his distance from her, but he wasn't doing a very good job of that. Still, he couldn't avoid her—even if he wanted to. She lived in his building, and he'd been asked to watch over her. Surely no harm could come in being friendly. He'd just have to make sure he didn't let what he felt for her go beyond that. But as Becca smiled up at him, he knew that was not going to be an easy feat. Not easy at all.

"Thank you for helping me the other night and for not letting everyone know how I almost caught the apartment on fire. I've had nightmares about setting the whole building on fire."

Luke shook his head. "I've had nightmares about *you* catching on fire."

"Oh dear, I am sorry. Only your quick thinking and actions prevented that."

"Well, let's put it out of our minds. Are you nervous about tomorrow?"

"I am, a little. But I'm excited, too. And I'm ready to go to work. I'm not used to. . .having all this time to myself."

"Are you homesick?" He certainly hoped not. He'd not like to see her go back to Eureka Springs.

"No. I miss my family, but I love the apartment. And I like Hot Springs better each day, although I haven't seen a lot of it yet. I probably used the wrong words. I should have said *leisure time*. I like being busy, and I love teaching."

"That's a very good thing for your students." The trolley stopped a block from the apartment building, and they got off and walked briskly down the street, as the night air had begun to cool quickly.

The night watchman greeted them as they entered the building. "Evening, Mr. Monroe, Miss Snow."

"I'll see Miss Snow to her apartment and be back down shortly, George." The watchman had noticed someone lurking around the other side of the street for several nights in a row and had told Luke that it seemed the man was watching their building. Luke wanted to know if he'd been back tonight, but he didn't want to mention it in front of Becca.

"You don't have to see me to my door," she said. "I'll be fine, and I'm sure you have things you need to do."

"Nothing that can't wait until I see you safely inside."

He walked her to the door and waited until she unlocked it and stepped inside. "I hope you have a very good day tomorrow. I look forward to hearing all about it."

"Thank you. I'm hoping it goes well, too. I'll let you know. Thank you for taking me to church and seeing me home."

"You're welcome. I can't see any reason for us to go separately when we're both going to the same place, can you?"

Becca shook her head. "It wouldn't make much sense, would it? But thank you anyway."

"You're welcome. I'll be waiting to hear how your first day goes. I'll wait for you to lock up. Good night."

"Good night," Becca said, shutting the door.

He heard the key turn in the lock before he headed back downstairs to talk to George. He prided himself that he kept this building safe, and he didn't like the idea that some stranger was watching the comings and goings of the tenants. The Wellington Building was known as one of the safest apartment buildings in the state, and he wanted to make sure it stayed that way.

❧

Abigail sat at her dressing table, brushing her hair while Marcus sat in front of the fire, reading. "Marcus, dear, did you notice the way Luke tried to keep from looking at Becca today?"

He chuckled. "No. I noticed how often he did look at her."

"You did notice, then. I think he's interested in her."

"It's about time he found someone. But I'm not sure Becca is ready. After losing her fiancé. . .you never know how long that might take."

Abigail sighed. "You are right. I wouldn't know what to do if something happened to you. Of course we are married, and Becca lost Richard before they married, but I don't know how much difference that would make."

Marcus shook his head. "No, neither do I. But in my mind, there is no doubt that Luke is interested in her. I think he's trying not to be, but as you and I both know, trying *not* to care for someone doesn't always work."

Abigail met her husband's eyes in the mirror and smiled.

"That is very true. I would hate for Luke to get hurt. I so want to see him happy. I think he longs for a family, for someone to love." She put her brush down, got up, and sat down beside her husband. He pulled her into his arms and kissed the top of her head.

"I'd like to see the same thing. And Becca is just the kind of woman he needs."

"Let's pray that her heart heals and that she is open to falling in love again—with Luke, of course."

"We can do that. You've turned into quite a romantic, my love."

"*You've* turned me into a romantic. And I just want to see Luke and Becca as happy as we are."

"That would be nice." Marcus tipped her head up and lowered his lips to hers.

"Mmm, yes, it would. . . ," Abigail said, just before his lips touched hers.

❧

Becca woke early the next day. She was both excited and apprehensive about her first day at Central High. She hoped her students liked her and that the other teachers were easy to get along with. She dressed with care in a brown and cream dress that made her feel businesslike. She pulled her hair up in a French twist, thinking it made her look older. Although she wanted to establish who was in charge from the very first, she preferred to do it by the way she handled herself, and she hoped by the end of the day her students would realize she was firm but fair.

Although she'd gone in and met Mr. Fuller, been shown

her room, and been given the curriculum the week before, he had asked her to come a little early today so that he could show her around more fully and introduce her to the other teachers. By the time she entered the school and made her way to the principal's office, she was pretty certain that she was much more nervous about meeting her students than they were about meeting her.

The secretary seemed pleased to see her again.

"Oh, I am so glad you are here, Miss Snow. It will be so nice to have Mr. Fuller in his office full-time so that I don't have to run down the hall every time I need to ask him about something or someone telephones him. I know he has been looking forward to this day, too."

She showed Becca into the principal's office right away, and Mr. Fuller stood as soon as she entered his office. It was obvious he was happy to be able to turn his class over to her, and he quickly put her at ease. "Miss Snow, I can't tell you how glad I am that you've decided to join our faculty. So are our teachers. They are eager to meet you. Come with me. They are waiting in the teachers' lounge."

He led her to a room just across from his office and introduced her. "This is Miss Becca Snow, who has come to relieve me in teaching the literature classes. Please make her feel welcome so that she will stay with us."

Everyone chuckled at his words, but she felt genuinely welcomed as he introduced her to each one. Becca knew she'd never remember all their names, but she tried to connect faces to names as she shook each hand.

The nice lady with hair that was graying was Mrs. Ella Richards, and she taught geography. The short blond who looked about the same age as Becca was named Lila Baxter, and she was the domestic science teacher. The redhead was Jennifer Collins, who taught Latin. Then there was Gene Landry, who taught algebra, and Harold Green, who taught geometry.

By the time she'd met the rest of the teachers, she was getting confused about who taught what but was assured she'd know them all better by the end of the week.

"Or next, anyway," Miss Collins said. "It took me two full weeks to get it all straight."

"And we'll help you remember. Don't worry at all if you call us by the wrong name," Miss Baxter added.

Everyone was so kind, offering to help in any way they could, that by the time Mr. Fuller took her to meet her students, Becca was sure she'd fit right in.

"I think you'll find the students are very easy to get along with and eager to learn," Mr. Fuller said as they walked up the stairs to the second floor. They passed several clusters of students, and Becca was pretty sure they knew she was the new teacher. Although they didn't speak, most of them smiled at her.

"I've enjoyed teaching them. It's just that I don't feel I'm doing justice to either them or my duties as principal. I think you'll enjoy the class, but if you have any concerns or questions, please don't hesitate to ask."

He stopped at a room at the end of the hall, and Becca was happy that there were so many windows and lots of light in the room. "I've left lesson plans for you for the next few weeks so that you didn't have to do all of that right away and you can see where we are."

"Oh thank you. That will help immensely."

"You're welcome. I know how hard it can be to step in

midyear. I really didn't think we'd find anyone this late in the year. I do hope you like it here, Miss Snow. I think you'll find the students are well behaved." He chuckled. "Most of them, anyway. I made up seating charts for each of your classes and will stay with you today to make sure no one tries to confuse you. Some of the boys certainly aren't above pulling a few pranks. I also made up a list of those I think might see how far they can push you in the first few weeks, and if one even tries, send them straight to me."

"Yes, sir. Don't worry. I will."

The bell rang, and true to his word, Mr. Fuller stayed with her, making sure everyone took the right seat. Then he introduced her.

"Class, this is your new teacher, Miss Snow. She's come all the way from Eureka Springs and is an excellent teacher. I'm sure you are going to find her much more pleasant to look at than me. Please make sure she doesn't regret her decision to move here."

Becca noticed that he smiled to take the sting out of his words before he cleared his throat and said, "I have enjoyed teaching each one of you this year. I believe you will all go far in life, and remember; I'll be watching to make sure you do. And just as it was here, my office door is always open to you."

It was obvious why he had such a good reputation as a principal. He deeply cared about each one of these young people. It appeared she had a lot to live up to in this class.

The morning passed quickly, and Becca enjoyed having lunch with the other teachers. If anything, the afternoon went by even faster, and by the time she caught a trolley back to the apartment, Becca was sure she was going to like teaching at Central High. For the most part, she didn't think she'd have any problems with her students. The girls all seemed very sweet and nice. The boys. . .were boys. Overall, they seemed well behaved, too, with the exception of two or three, and she thought they were just a little mischievous. Time would tell.

Burrows had been watching the Wellington Building for days and only this morning had seen the woman come out and take the trolley. He stepped on the trolley at the back, took a seat, and unfolded the newspaper he'd brought with him. He pretended to read while he waited to find out what stop she would get off at. It was near the end of the line when she stepped off and headed toward the high school.

Hmm. Apparently she was a teacher. He couldn't remember any teachers he'd met recently. He had to find out where he'd run into her. For some reason, he hadn't been able to get the young woman out of his mind. But perhaps it wasn't here. He was out of town a lot in his line of business. Maybe she'd just moved here. But how was he to find out? Maybe he could pretend to be interested in renting an apartment in the building. That was it. He'd walk right in and talk to the manager. He had business to attend to, but he'd go there this afternoon. Perhaps he'd see the young woman again and remember where it was he'd seen her before. It was imperative that he find out.

At two thirty Burrows rode the trolley back to the Wellington Building and walked right in as if he had every right to be there. The day watchman looked up from his desk. "May I help you, sir?"

"Yes. My name is Harland Burrows, and I'd like to talk to the manager about renting an apartment. I've heard good things about this building."

"I don't believe we have any openings right now, but you can talk to Mr. Monroe. He might put you on a waiting list. I can see if he has time to see you now, if you'd like."

"Yes, I would. Thank you." This might be easier than he had thought.

The guard picked up the telephone, and in minutes Burrows was shown to the manager's office.

"Mr. Monroe, this is Mr. Burrows. I told him I didn't think we had any openings, but he'd like to talk to you about putting his name on the waiting list."

"Come in, Mr. Burrows," the building manager said. "Derrick is right. We have no openings at present, but you can put your name on a list. That won't guarantee that you will get an apartment or when one might become available. What it will guarantee is that we will get in touch with you if your name is next on the list when we have a vacancy. Would you like to do that?"

"Yes, I believe I would."

"I'd need you to fill out an application." Mr. Monroe handed him a form to fill out.

Harland looked it over and began to fill it out.

"Would it be possible for me to see an apartment or floor plan?"

"I have a floor plan I could show you. Would you be needing a one- or two-bedroom apartment?"

"Perhaps a two-bedroom. I'm out of town often on business. The wife likes to have her family come to visit occasionally, especially when I am gone."

Mr. Monroe slid a floor plan of the building over to him. Harland couldn't ask for anything more. It gave the room numbers of each apartment and the layout. The building manager pointed to an apartment in the middle of the building. "This would be a two-bedroom floor plan. They are all alike but could be reversed, depending on which one became vacant."

Harland looked it over. Obviously they were very nice apartments—much nicer than what he was renting now. But what he really paid attention to were the room numbers. Apartment 312 was a corner apartment looking out over Central Avenue. That was what he'd wanted to know. "These are very nice."

"Yes, they are the nicest apartments in town. We don't have an empty one for long."

Harland stood up, hoping to take the floor plan with him, but Mr. Monroe held out his hand. "I'm afraid I need that back. It's the master copy, and it stays here."

"Yes, of course." He didn't really need it. He'd seen enough. "Thank you. I look forward to getting that call one of these days."

"Good day, Mr. Burrows."

Harland left the office and turned just in time to see the young woman come through the door. When she looked at him and he met her gaze, he was even more positive that he had seen her before. But where? He pulled his hat down low and hurried out the door. He had better find out, and the sooner the better.

seven

By the time Becca stepped off the trolley and entered the apartment building, she realized just how very tired she was. She didn't know if she had the energy to make even a light supper.

A man came out of Luke's office just then, and Becca thought he looked familiar. When he pulled his hat down over his eyes, she remembered where she'd seen him. It was at the grocer's the day she'd moved in. But she'd thought he looked familiar then, too. She sighed. Well, he would this time. After all, she'd run into him twice already.

Luke came out of his office just as she reached the elevator.

"Who is that man?"

"He's Harland Burrows. He came to inquire about an apartment. Why?"

"Oh, I've just run into him before, and he looks very familiar to me. But I don't recognize the name." She smiled and shrugged. "He probably just looks like someone I've met before."

Luke nodded. "That happens to me, too. How did your first day go, Becca?"

"It went very well, thank you. But I'm quite tired. I must have become lazy during the last few weeks. I'd forgotten how much energy it takes keeping up with high school students. They are very bright, and they ask a lot of questions."

"Why don't you let me treat you to dinner then? Don't you

think you should celebrate your first day teaching here?"

"Oh, I can't let you do that."

"Why not?"

"You just took me out to dinner the night of the fire."

"I'm not talking about taking you to dinner. I'm talking about making you dinner. I'll bring it to you."

"You will make me dinner?" His thoughtfulness touched her heart, and she could hear her voice soften. "That would be nice. But only if you let me return the favor soon."

He smiled. "I rarely turn down a dinner invitation, Becca. Of course I'll let you return the favor. I'm roasting a chicken. I'll bring it over about six. Just set a table for us."

"All right. Thank you. I wasn't looking forward to frying eggs again." Suddenly Becca wasn't quite so tired. She found herself looking forward to dinner with Luke and to having someone to talk with about her day.

༄

Becca set the round table in front of the bay window with the china and crystal she'd brought over from the Wellingtons' and the silverware her mother had sent. She'd been filling a hope chest for years, but after setting up housekeeping here, she'd realized that she hadn't accumulated anywhere near as much as she thought she had for her marriage to Richard. Of course there would have been wedding gifts, and they would have bought things to fill out what they didn't have, but Becca realized that it was over years that people accumulated all they needed to live in the lifestyle she now enjoyed due primarily to her family and the Wellingtons.

While she waited for Luke, she made iced tea and straightened the already-neat parlor before going to the bathroom to freshen up. She still found it hard to believe that she was living in such a nice place. She dampened her comb and ran it over her hair, straightening the wayward curls that liked to spring up around her face.

Each time she came into this room, she almost felt guilty. Until a year or so before, she and her mother had been using an outdoor privy. Meagan and Nate had practically begged her mother to let them put a real bathroom in, such as they had in their new home. Finally, with a little help from the urging of Becca and Sarah, Mama had given in.

Becca decided to count herself blessed that she was able to live in such a fine fashion, but at the same time, she felt quite spoiled. She prayed she'd never take all this for granted.

A knock on the door had her hurrying through the apartment to answer it. Luke was standing there with a grin on his face and a huge picnic basket on his arm. "At your service, miss. May I ask where you would like me to set up our meal?"

He grinned and raised an eyebrow, and Becca couldn't help but laugh. She motioned to the table. "Right over there. I thought it would be nicer than the dining room. It's a little formal, and this is more—"

"This is just right. I don't have a table like this, but I have a chair in my bay window, and it's where I usually eat, too. Dining rooms are nice if you are having more than two people to dine, but with two people, one at each end of a long table, it seems. . ."

Too far away was Becca's first thought, but instead she said, "A long way to pass the potatoes. I'm not sure either of us has arms long enough for that."

Luke threw back his head and laughed. "You are absolutely right. But how did you know I brought creamed potatoes?"

"I didn't, but those are my favorite kind. Let me help you get this on the table. My mouth is watering at the aroma." She helped him set out the roast chicken, potatoes, and peas. He filled their plates while she poured iced tea into the goblets. Then she took her seat, and Luke said a blessing before they began to eat.

Becca took her first bite and closed her eyes. "This is delicious. I can't believe you cooked all of this. But oh, thank you. I am getting so tired of the few things I know how to cook."

"You really don't know how to cook? Or are you just frightened after the grease fire?"

"A little of both, I suppose, but mostly the latter." Feeling the need to explain about her lack of cooking skills, she added, "My older sisters helped Mama in the kitchen the most. I set the table and did the dishes a lot, but I seemed to have missed out on learning all Mama could have taught me."

"I'll show you how to safely light the burners and the oven. And I'll be glad to teach you what I know about cooking."

Becca nodded. "I'll take you up on the offer. I'm going to pick up a copy of Fannie Farmer's book, too, this weekend. I meant to do that on the way home today, but I was so tired that I forgot."

Luke nodded. "It would be good to have. But there is no need to hurry. I can help you this week. It would probably be better to work in your kitchen so that you know where everything is and how your range works. After we eat, I can see what you have on hand, and we'll make up a menu for the next few days. Then I'll come over and help. Don't worry about what you don't have. If we're going to eat our cooking together, I can buy what we need."

Becca thought her mother would disapprove of her having Luke over so often. It might not have been approved behavior when Mama was young, but it was 1902, after all.

She took another bite of chicken. If she could learn to cook even half as well as this, she would be quite comfortable asking people over for dinner. And she was bound to want to, once she got to know more people from her new church family and the high school faculty—not to mention the Wellingtons and Luke.

Besides, Luke had never treated her in any inappropriate way. He'd been helpful and friendly, but she would expect nothing less from the manager of the building and the employee of the Wellingtons. In fact, several times she'd wondered if he was only nice to her for those reasons. She'd hoped that he liked her for herself, and she had begun to think of him as a friend she could talk to, someone she could count on.

She wasn't totally comfortable with the way her heart jumped when he smiled at her. Or the way she looked forward to seeing him each day. But Luke didn't know how he made her feel, and at any rate, he seemed to be only acting out of kindness and friendship. At the moment, that was exactly what she needed.

"Thank you, Luke. If I ever get to the point that I can make chicken taste this good by myself, I'll cook the whole dinner for you."

"I'll certainly agree to that, Becca. What time would you like me to come over tomorrow?"

"Whenever you need to. You know how long it takes to prepare a meal. I still don't know how you time it all to be ready at the same time."

"You will. I'll be here around five thirty."

They finished the meal, talking about what Becca had on hand and what they could make, then Luke helped her clear the table, gathering his dishes to take home. But Becca wasn't about to let him take home dirty dishes. The least she could do was wash them for him. She did that while he took stock of her pantry.

They worked in silence, her washing and drying dishes and repacking his basket and him making a list of menus for the week. It was a comfortable feeling. . .not awkward at all. *Yes,* she thought, *right now Luke is just the person I need to be around—a friend who expects only friendship in return.* She found herself looking forward to the next day—not just because of her new job but because she would be able to spend the evening with Luke.

❧

Becca's day went very well on Tuesday. She began to think she might be able to put names to faces fairly soon, thanks to Mr. Fuller's seating chart. His lesson plans would prove to be invaluable to her also. These first few weeks would be much easier if she didn't have to create her own plans. It would give her time to assess where her class as a whole was and how fast she could expect them to move through the material she had left to teach for the year.

She was finding that being in a new school in a new town, meeting new people, and learning the rules and regulations she was expected to observe at school, while exciting, was a bit more tiring than she'd thought it would be. Actually she hadn't thought about the adjustments she'd be making when she decided to move. All she'd wanted to do was get away from painful memories.

She hadn't been able to escape them altogether, but she'd had so many new experiences that thoughts of what could have been didn't come quite so often, and when they did, she got busy with something that took her mind off it all. And yet, she felt guilty that she wasn't thinking of Richard quite as much these days. She knew she'd loved him, and the heartache she'd suffered had been deep and lasting—so much so that she didn't know if she would ever be able to fall in love again. Certainly she didn't want to give her heart to anyone who had a dangerous position: not another policeman, not a fireman, not anyone who put his life on the line by choice.

But the memory of what Richard looked like had begun to fade, and she had to pull out a photo of him to remember. Yet what good did that do? It only served to make her sad. He wasn't here, and the life they'd planned could never be. In the last few months Becca had come to accept that fact. Now she found she was longing to look forward to the future once more.

And today she was anticipating her first cooking lesson from Luke. She could just imagine what her mother would have to say about it. As she stepped off the trolley and walked the short way to the Wellington Building, she chuckled. She wasn't sure that was something she wanted to share with her mother. . .not just yet anyway.

She hurried up to her apartment and unlocked the door. As she walked in, she found a note had been slipped under her door. She picked it up and read the masculine handwriting. "I'll be a little late. I'm picking up a few things at the grocer's. You can peel a couple of potatoes, cut them into cubes, and put them in a pan of water, if you'd like."

"I should be able to do that," Becca said out loud. She changed into a dress more appropriate for cooking and put on one of the aprons her mother had sent from home. By the time Luke knocked on the door, she was feeling quite domestic.

She opened the door to him and found that he had his arms full. "Oh, Luke, what have you got there?"

"You were a little short on a few things, and if we're going to be cooking, I wanted to make sure you had everything we might need."

"I bought the staples Mama always said to have on hand: flour, sugar, salt, and pepper."

"Your mother was right. But you also need baking powder and soda and some spices for flavoring."

Becca led him to the kitchen and helped him unload his bags. As she pulled out nutmeg, cinnamon, ginger, and cloves, she could remember her mother using them back home. She just wasn't sure in what dishes the different spices were used. How could she have lived in that home for all those years and not learned to cook more than she did? Well, she was going to learn now. That was all there was to it.

She turned to Luke. "What do you need me to do?"

❧

Becca looked adorable in her ruffled apron. She could just stand there looking pretty and talk to Luke while he cooked for her if she wanted to. But she really did seem to want to learn to cook. From her talk of her mother cooking and her sister helping with her education, he didn't think that she'd been raised in the same kind of luxury Abigail had been. He was certain that she came from an upstanding family, but he vaguely remembered that they had fallen on hard times at some point and that was why her sister had gone into the dressmaking business.

Perhaps the fact that she came from that upbringing was why he related to her so well. . .but none of that changed the fact that he had no business dreaming of her at night or thinking of her first thing in the morning. He shouldn't have offered to help her learn to cook, but he wasn't going to back out now, not when she was looking at him so expectantly.

"You have the potatoes ready to boil. We'll drain most of the water and add butter and parsley to them once they are done." He put the pot on the range and showed her how to operate the damper to control the amount of heat. "I'm sure you know how to do this—"

"No, that's not the way I was doing it. This range is a little different from the one at home." She watched him closely. "I'll try to remember how you did it."

"I can show you again anytime." He turned toward her. "Once the potatoes come to a boil, we'll move them to a cooler spot and let them simmer. Then I'll let you be in charge of them."

"I think I can manage. What are we having with them? I have some bacon—"

"We'll save that for another night. I bought a couple of pork chops. We're starting fairly easy and are just going to fry them."

"Mmm, I do like pork chops," Becca said as she watched him unwrap the white butcher paper to reveal two thick chops.

"But first we're going to mix up some biscuits."

"Oh my. Biscuits—I'm not sure that's starting out easy."

"They aren't hard. You'll see." He pulled a piece of paper

out of his pocket. "Here is an easy biscuit recipe. We'll need a bowl and two cups of flour measured into it."

Becca pulled out a bowl and her measuring cups. She carefully measured the flour into the bowl.

"Now we need four teaspoons of baking powder and a half teaspoon of salt. I'll make sure the oven is hot enough while you are doing that."

"And now what?"

"Now you cut up two tablespoons butter into the flour mixture."

"Oh, I remember Mama doing that. She used two forks." Becca pulled two out of a drawer, and after putting two cubes of butter in the bowl with the flour mixture, she began pulling the forks in opposite directions across the butter.

"That's how I do it."

"Milk next?" Becca smiled up at him.

"You do remember. Yes, a cup. We're going to make it easy and just drop them onto a buttered pan. Next time we'll roll them out. Don't add the milk just yet, though. I need to get the chops started. Where is a skillet?"

Becca pulled one out of the cupboard and handed it to him. Luke took the skillet and put it on a burner, then he carefully slid the chops into the skillet and seasoned them with salt and pepper. "We'll have to watch them closely so they don't burn. Once they are browned, we'll let them cook slowly. The potatoes are boiling, so you can move the pot over to the side of the burner so they can simmer."

Becca did as he suggested, and the rolling boil quickly settled down to a gentle simmer. "Do I add the butter now?"

She really was eager to learn, and it made him more determined to teach her. "Not yet. We'll do that a little later.

Part of putting a meal on the table and having everything ready at one time depends on learning how long each thing takes to cook. Mostly it just takes practice."

"How do you know when to turn the pork chops over?"

"You can lift a corner and see how it is doing. Or you can nudge it like this." Luke pushed at one of the chops with his fork, and it didn't want to move. "It needs a little more time."

"What about those biscuits? Should I add the milk and drop them on the pan?"

"Yes, please. I'll watch the chops." But he also watched Becca. She was concentrating so hard on mixing the dough that she seemed unaware of his presence. Then she turned around and found him looking at her.

"Ah, is the dough ready to drop?" she asked, delicate color flooding her cheeks.

"Yes, I think so. You can put them on the pan." He turned back and checked the chops. This time the chop slid easily, so he turned it over and did the same with the second one. He was thankful that he hadn't let them burn while he was watching Becca.

"I think this is the way my mother did it when she was in a hurry," Becca said, taking a spoonful and dropping it onto the pan by pushing it off the spoon with her finger.

"I'd say she probably did. You are doing fine." He checked the chops and moved them to a slower-cooking burner. "Now we'll let the chops cook slowly while the biscuits bake."

Becca nodded as she dropped the last biscuit onto the pan. "I think they are ready."

Luke opened the oven door so she could slip the pan in. "Now we can butter the potatoes. I brought a can of peas we can heat up, too."

Becca brought out another pan, and Luke opened the peas and dumped them into it. "We can heat these up and add a little butter to them. Mama didn't add much else, if I remember right."

"You can be in charge of them while I show you how to butter the potatoes," Luke said. He drained most of the water off them, salted and peppered them, and then added some butter before putting them back over a low fire. He chopped some parsley and added that to the pan. "The water and butter will cook down and make a good sauce while the parsley will give a little more flavor and add some color."

"Everything smells wonderful. I'll fill our glasses and take them to the table, along with the butter. Would you like some honey to go with the biscuits?"

"Yes, please. The chops are almost done, and I think the biscuits are, too." When Becca came back from setting things on the table, he asked, "What do you want me to put them in?" Had he been by himself, he would have just slapped it all on a plate and been done with it, but he didn't suggest that approach.

"Well, I know it's not the way we'd be doing it at the Wellingtons'—or even at home, for that matter—but why don't we just fill our plates and take them to the table? I have a basket we can use for the biscuits."

She was a woman after his own heart. "That's how I'd do it if I were at home."

"Well, I probably should have it set up all proper and everything, but right now just getting it on the table seems a great accomplishment."

"That's how I feel after working all day." Luke pulled out the biscuits that had baked to a golden brown, and then he dished up the chops while Becca added potatoes and peas to each plate. "And you've done great tonight. The biscuits smell wonderful. Next time I'll let you fry the chops."

"Oh, you will?" Becca smiled at him from over her shoulder as she headed for the parlor with her plate and the basket of biscuits.

If he didn't know better, he'd think she was being flirtatious. But she'd given him no indication that she thought of him in that way. None at all. Luke sighed and followed her out of the kitchen.

❧

Becca bowed her head while Luke said a prayer over their meal. She tried to concentrate on what he was saying instead of thinking how handsome he'd looked in her kitchen. She hadn't been prepared for the way she felt just having him in the small area, as they'd moved around each other while they worked together. It was quite enjoyable, and she was very proud of the meal she and Luke had prepared. He had done most of the work, but he'd let her do enough that she felt as if she truly had cooked. . .and cooked well. The biscuits were light and fluffy and tasted as good as any she'd eaten. She was looking forward to rolling them out next time so that they looked as good, too.

"Mmm, the pork chops are just how I like them."

"They are good, aren't they?" Luke agreed with a smile. "But not as good as your biscuits. How do you like the potatoes?"

"Thank you. About the biscuits, I mean. I like the potatoes, and I think I could make them on my own."

"You can do this whole meal on your own. I'll leave the biscuit recipe with you, just so you have it to go by."

"I think that is part of the problem. I didn't write things down while my mother was trying to teach me. But the real issue is that I mostly watched and didn't do."

"Well, you are going to do fine, because I'm going to let you do most of it."

Becca took another bite of pork chop. It was very good: crisp on the outside, moist on the inside, and seasoned just right. "I hope you don't expect anything this good—at least not just yet."

She looked out the window and thought she saw someone under the light across the street looking up, but when she stared more carefully, the person had moved on. She didn't know if she'd imagined it or not, but for several evenings she'd thought the same thing. She shook her head and sighed.

"What is it?"

"Nothing really. I just thought I saw someone outside looking up this way. It's probably just my imagination."

Luke looked out the window. "Was it a man or woman?"

"A man. The last few evenings I've thought someone was watching from across the street, but when I looked again, he was always on his way up the street. Besides, it's no crime to look up at a building. I do it, too. I'm sure it was just my imagination." She felt a little silly even bringing it up.

"Well, it might be, but it never hurts to be sure. Don't hesitate to let me know if you think someone is watching your windows again. The Wellington is a safe place to live, and I want to keep it that way. But we need to know if that reputation is threatened in any way. Don't ever feel anything that bothers you is too small to tell me."

Luke made her feel much better, but still she wanted to change the subject. She didn't like the idea that someone might be out there watching her windows. "I'm sorry I don't have anything for dessert."

"With biscuits as light as these and butter and honey, who needs a fancy dessert?" Luke said, making her feel as if he couldn't want for more. By the time she saw him to the door after he insisted on helping to clean up the kitchen, Becca was beginning to think this man was too good to be real.

eight

By that Thursday Becca had learned how to roll and cut out biscuits and make mayonnaise and chicken salad—on Wednesday they'd used the leftover chicken from Monday night—and tonight she'd learned to make an omelet and fry bacon without burning it. All in all she thought she was off to a good start. Well, she had burned the first few pieces of bacon, but Luke had showed her how to regulate the heat again, and the next batch was cooked just right.

When he'd left that night, he'd said, "Tomorrow is Friday, and. . .I. . .ah. . .I know that we aren't sweethearts, but it is Valentine's Day, and well, you are new in town, and I think we should celebrate a week of you learning how to cook. Will you let me take you to dinner?"

She'd been trying hard not to think about the next day being Valentine's Day. But she hadn't been able to banish it from her thoughts entirely, and she'd dreaded spending the evening alone, thinking about Richard and what could have been had he lived. Luke's invitation would enable her to spend the evening in the company of someone besides herself, and she was thankful for it.

Becca's heart seemed to do a little dive into her stomach as she watched the color rise on Luke's cheeks while he waited for her answer. Why, he was unsure of what she would say. While they weren't sweethearts, they'd become friends, and it would be a whole lot less lonesome if they spent the evening together. "That would be very nice, Luke. Thank you."

Over the last few evenings she'd found that she liked the man very much. . .and could be in danger of losing her heart to him if she wasn't very careful. Now as she dressed for her dinner with Luke, she took care with her hair and wore a dinner dress that she'd worn only once before, but she loved it. It was a Worth-inspired gown of red silk with black trim. Her sister was such a wonderful seamstress that Becca was sure many would think it was an original Worth gown. She was just glad that she didn't have to pay the Worth price.

She felt wonderful, and when she opened the door to Luke a few minutes later, his expression told her what he thought before he spoke. "What a beautiful gown," Luke said. "You look lovely tonight, Becca."

"Thank you, Luke. You look very nice, too." He had on a black overcoat with a black fur collar over a black suit, a wing-collared shirt, and a black silk tie. He didn't just look nice; he looked quite handsome.

He helped her on with her black cloak trimmed in fur and then pulled something red out of his pocket. "This is just because I wanted to give you something to celebrate your first week of teaching and how well you are doing with your cooking. You can open it later if you want." He handed the prettily wrapped package to her.

She took it and turned it over in her hand. "Oh, Luke, you shouldn't have. But since you did, may I open it now?"

"Of course you may."

Becca tore open the wrapping to find not candy as she'd expected but a leather copy of Fannie Farmer's cookbook. "Oh, Luke, thank you. I was going to pick up a copy tomorrow."

"I know. But I wanted to get it for you. It seemed fitting

since I'm helping you learn to cook. Besides, I figured I could learn a few things, too."

"I know I can learn a lot from it. We'll go over it later." Becca laid it on the table in the bay window. "Thank you so much. I can't wait to use it."

She knew they weren't sweethearts, but when Luke locked the door for her and cupped her elbow with his hand as they walked to the elevator, she felt more special than she had in a very long time. He'd hired a hack to take them to the restaurant instead of taking the trolley, and that only added to the special feel of the evening.

He'd made reservations at the Park Hotel. Its dining room was quite beautiful, with windows on three sides. It was said to be one of the nicest in the city. They were shown to a table for two, and on this night in particular, Becca was glad to have Luke as an escort. The room was full of couples, the ladies dressed in their finest and the men dressed much like Luke.

They were handed menus, and Becca looked over the choices. They seemed very expensive, and she wasn't sure what Luke could afford. "Would you order for me? I don't know what is best."

"I'd be glad to. Their fillet of beef is excellent. It's served with potato croquettes and peas, but the meal starts off with mock turtle soup and ends with ice cream and nut cake."

"It all sounds wonderful."

Luke nodded, and the waiter seemed to appear out of nowhere. Luke gave him the order, and he left as quietly as he'd come.

"How did your day go?" Luke asked.

Becca knew he would raise this question, for he'd asked her each day this week when he'd come for a cooking lesson. "It was very nice. The school held a secret Valentine exchange. During lunchtime the students could go into each room and put a card on the other desks, just one or all of them. But they had to take turns. I ate my lunch at my desk and made sure that only one student at a time came in. Then right before the last class was dismissed, they could open their cards. Some had more than others, but everyone got several, and they all seemed quite happy."

"Good. I would hope no one was left out," Luke said. "So overall do you think you are going to like teaching there?"

Becca nodded. "I already do. I'm glad I made the move. I needed—"

The waiter chose that moment to bring their soup, and Becca was glad of the interruption. It had been a lovely evening, and there was no need to put a damper on it by bringing up Richard's death.

As soon as the waiter left the table, Luke said, "Please pray with me." He bowed his head and prayed. "Dear Lord, we thank You for this day and that it was a good one for Becca. Thank You for the beautiful day You've blessed us with, and help us to live each day to Your glory. We thank You for the food we are about to eat. Most of all, we thank You for our salvation through Your Son and our Savior. It is in His name we pray. Amen."

They began eating their soup, and talk turned to cooking. "Thank you again for the cookbook. I'd like to have the Wellingtons over for dinner once I learn to cook a little better."

"That won't be long. You are a fast learner. I looked through Mrs. Farmer's book, and the instructions seem very clear and easy to follow."

Becca chuckled. "That's what I need. How did *you* learn to

cook so well? Did your mother teach you?"

"I learned some from her, but she died when I was young. Actually, I learned most of what I know from the Wellingtons' cook. When I liked something, I asked how to make it, and she was always willing to tell me. I have a box full of recipes. Sometimes I'd go into the kitchen while she was making a meal and she would show me what to do."

He told her of several disasters in his kitchen. "I might not have caught my kitchen on fire, but I've burned several things to a crisp. The first chicken I tried to roast shriveled on its bones, and I caught a steak just before it burst into flames."

By the time they'd finished their meal, Becca's sides were sore from laughing. It had been a very long time since she'd enjoyed an evening as much as this one. When Luke smiled at her from across the table, her pulse began to race, and she wondered if perhaps her heart was on the mend after all.

Suddenly she wanted to know all about Luke: where he was born, how he came to work for Marcus, why he hadn't married and had a family yet. But it wasn't until they were on their way back to the apartments that she got up enough nerve to ask about him.

"I'm sorry about your mother, Luke. Is your father alive? Do you have any siblings?"

"No, I have no brothers or sisters, and my father died several years ago."

"Are you from Hot Springs?"

"No. I was born in Fort Smith. But once I went to work for Marcus, I moved here. I consider Hot Springs my home now."

"It does seem to be a nice place to live. I think I'll be considering it home before long, too. How did you come to work for Marcus?"

"Oh, I met him not long after I left home, years ago. He took pity on the young man I was and offered me a job working for him. I owe Marcus a great deal. I've never doubted that I made the right decision—not once in all these years."

She didn't have enough nerve to ask why he'd never married. Instead she decided she was just glad he hadn't.

As they finished their ride home in the quiet of the hack, Becca thanked the Lord above that she'd found a real friend in Hot Springs. Luke had helped her feel at home here, keeping her from being terribly homesick. This might not have been the kind of Valentine's Day most women dreamed about, but she would always remember it as one of the most special she would ever have.

❧

Luke thought back over the evening and realized that he could tell himself that he and Becca Snow were just friends all he wanted; he'd be lying to himself, as it was all he could do to keep from pulling her into his arms when he said good night.

Yet after the questions she'd asked, he was more convinced than ever that he had to stop the growing feelings he had for her. He hadn't been able to tell her that he'd gotten in with the wrong crowd and ended up in jail for a crime he hadn't committed. He hadn't been able to bring himself to tell her that he met Marcus when the man had gotten him out of jail all those years ago. He hadn't been able to tell her that he owed Marcus Wellington his very life.

He'd been afraid she'd look at him with disdain in her eyes, and he didn't think he could bear that. And even if she didn't reject him, she was a lovely, wonderful woman who came from a very good family. Once they found out, he was sure they would discourage her from having anything to do with him. Then there was the age difference. While he had no doubt that she thought of him as a friend, he was sure she wouldn't be thinking of him as a suitor—and deep down, that was really what he wanted to be.

He shouldn't be spending as much time with her as he was. Instead he should be distancing himself from her. But that was the last thing he wanted to do.

Yet he should tell her about his past—he knew he should tell her. And he would. . .soon.

ِ

Over the next month Becca and Luke got to know each other even better. When they were spending two or three evenings a week together with her cooking lessons, it seemed the most natural thing to accompany each other to church and then to the Wellingtons' on Sundays.

Luke never failed to ask how her day went at school, and Becca had come to look forward to talking over the day with him and asking about his. From what he told her, he stayed busy running the building and helping Marcus with various projects from time to time. With Luke's help and her new cookbook, Becca was beginning to feel she could ask the Wellingtons over soon. Maybe she would start with some of the teachers at school.

Tonight she and Luke were making Maryland Chicken using a recipe from the cookbook he'd bought her. It was fairly easy, and while it cooked, Luke made a salad and Becca made biscuits. She was quite proud that she could roll them out now and that they were as light as a feather.

She'd put green beans on earlier, seasoning them with

bacon grease, onion, and garlic like her mother's recipe called for—one from a batch of recipes in the last letter her mother had sent. Becca found she liked cooking very much, and she pored over her new cookbook, looking for things to try.

"Now that spring is almost here, how are your students doing?" Luke asked. "Have they been up to any antics?"

"No. None that I know of, anyway." Becca liked teaching at Central High more each week. Her students were getting used to the way she did things, and they all seemed to like her.

He chuckled. "Well, be on the watch. If my memory serves me, spring is when young men seem to want to pull a few pranks."

Luke took the chicken out of the oven, and Becca slid her biscuits in the oven beside the potatoes so they'd be ready at the same time. "I'll be on guard. Oh! Have you heard about an alligator farm that is being made? That's been all the talk at school. The teachers have been talking about taking an outing with the students once it's up and running."

"I have heard about that. It's going to be out on Whittington Avenue. I've driven by there a few times. The city council decided to let it come in to give tourists who come to Bathhouse Row something else to do for entertainment."

"Hmm. I'm not sure watching alligators is what I would choose to do, but my students are all excited about it. I don't know exactly where it is. I know my way around this area, and I know how to get to church, school, and the Wellingtons', but there is a lot I still haven't seen of Hot Springs."

"The weather is getting better each day. Perhaps we can go for a drive on Sunday afternoon. I'll take you around and show you where the alligator farm will be and all the other places you haven't seen yet."

"That would be quite nice. I'd like that, thank you."

By now, she and Luke had a routine of setting the table together and going back to the kitchen to fill up their plates. When the biscuits were done, Luke dished up the chicken while Becca added the green beans and croquettes to the plates. Then he took the plates to the table by the bay window, and she brought in the biscuits.

He pulled out Becca's chair and seated her before taking the one across from her. He said a blessing before the meal, and Becca realized that it was the evenings they cooked together and shared a meal that she enjoyed the very best.

Besides Sunday dinner at the Wellingtons', she and Abigail had lunch together most Saturdays, and occasionally she'd been invited to a dinner party at their home. But it was these weeknights she shared with Luke that she looked forward to the most, and she knew that her life would be very lonely without his company. But she was afraid she'd become too dependent on him.

She looked over to find his gaze on her. "What is it?"

"I don't think you are going to need many more lessons. You are becoming quite a good cook, Becca."

She could feel the color flood her cheeks at his compliment. "Thank you. But I still have a lot to learn. Besides, how will I know how I'm doing if I don't have someone to try out my cooking?"

Luke grinned and shook his head. "Oh, I didn't say I wouldn't be here. . .just that I think you've learned about all I can teach you. I think I'll be learning from you from now on."

"I think we'll both be learning from Fannie Farmer."

"I do believe you are ready to have the Wellingtons or anyone else you'd like to have over whenever you wish." He took a bite of chicken.

"I've been thinking about that. I thought I might have some of the female teachers over one night before I ask the Wellingtons."

"I think that's a very good idea."

"Maybe I'll ask them for Saturday evening. But what will you do?"

"The same thing I did before you came into my life. I'll have dinner out."

"That sounds lonesome." She hated to think of him being alone. Of course they didn't eat every meal together, but they did it often enough so that she felt bad for having a dinner party without him.

"Sometimes it was. But you need to be doing things with people your age. I shouldn't be monopolizing all your time."

"My age! Age doesn't matter, and I haven't noticed a difference. Luke, I wouldn't even be thinking about having anyone over if it weren't for you. You've given me the confidence to do it."

Luke didn't quite seem himself tonight. Over the last day or two he'd seemed a little different, and Becca couldn't quite put her finger on what it was. Perhaps he was tired of spending so much time with her. Maybe he thought she was too immature for him. Those thoughts had her heart twisting in her chest, and Becca suddenly realized that she was very close to falling in love with Luke. But he hadn't given her any indication that he might care for her in that way, and from his conversation tonight, he seemed to want to distance himself from her.

"Luke, have I done something to upset you?"

"Of course not. Why would you ask?"

She shrugged. "It just seems as though you. . .maybe I've been monopolizing *your* time. I suppose I have. You had a life before I moved here, but I haven't let you live it. I'm sorry, Luke."

"Becca, you are talking nonsense. I didn't have much of a life before you moved here. But I'm ten years older than you are, and my life is what it is. You've begun a new life here and are just getting to know other people. I don't want you worrying about me just because you want to have your friends over for dinner or you want to go out with them. But you haven't done anything to upset me."

Becca knew Luke was trying to reassure her, but instead she felt more unsettled than before. There was something in the tone of his voice that didn't match the words he was saying, and she had to force herself to finish her meal. Something was wrong. She just didn't know what it was.

nine

Luke woke in the middle of the night. Or rather he gave up trying to sleep. All he'd been doing was tossing and turning. The evening had started out wonderful, and the meal had turned out delicious. But something had gone wrong somewhere during his and Becca's conversation, and he wasn't sure what it was or exactly when it had happened.

He couldn't figure out why Becca thought she might have upset him in some way, and when she'd asked about it, it was all Luke had been able to do to keep from pulling her in his arms to assure her that she hadn't. But he didn't have that right, and he was afraid that such a gesture might end their friendship forever. While he could never hope to win Becca's love, he wanted her friendship. She'd livened up his life more than she would ever know, and the thought of not having her in it was something he just didn't want to think about.

Still, he didn't think his words had convinced her that she hadn't done anything to upset him, and he wasn't sure he hadn't made things worse. She'd seemed quieter for the rest of the evening. While they had talked about this and that, it wasn't the easy conversation they'd had earlier, and he'd taken his leave a little earlier than usual.

He was upset with himself—for letting himself fall in love with her, for letting himself look forward to any time at all in her company, and for beginning to dream that she might someday return his feelings.

He knew better—especially if she ever learned of his past. He needed to distance himself from her, now more than ever. But he didn't want to. . .didn't think it was possible that he even could.

⁂

By Sunday things seemed back to normal with Luke, and Becca was relieved. True to his word, he'd telephoned her after her dinner guests had left on Saturday night to find out how it went.

Her heart had skipped a beat when she heard his voice, and it did the same now when she met him in the lobby to go to church. His smile seemed genuine, and she wanted nothing more than to believe that everything was all right as they headed outside to catch the trolley.

She'd dressed with care in her favorite green silk Sunday dress. It had pleats down each side of the flat front and the back, which had a small train. She brought her parasol along and a matching reticule.

"It's going to be a beautiful day. Are you ready for a little sightseeing after lunch?"

For the first time that morning Becca breathed easy. He hadn't mentioned the planned outing last night, and she'd thought he might have forgotten or decided that it wasn't a good idea. "I am looking forward to it very much. Do you think Abigail and Marcus might join us?"

"I don't know. We'll have to see if they have others over." He put his hand on her elbow to assist her in stepping up into the trolley and followed her down the aisle.

Becca sat next to the window and thought she saw the man who seemed so familiar to her across the street. "Isn't that the man who wants to rent an apartment in the building?"

Luke leaned in front of her to look out, but by then the man had pulled his hat down over his eyes and was walking down the street. "It might be. I'm not sure." He settled back down in his seat, and Becca released the breath she'd been holding. His nearness had her heart beating so fast she could barely breathe.

Seemingly unaware of the effect he had on her, Luke kept talking. "We aren't going to have any openings for a while. Well, there is one that might come open in a few months, but Marcus asked me to hold it in case Natalie moves here. And even if she doesn't, Mr. Burrows's name isn't that high up on the list. We have quite a long one."

"How did I get in so easily?"

"Marcus asked me to hold it for you."

"How nice the Wellingtons are." She owed them for more than their hospitality. She owed them for making it possible to get to know this wonderful man.

"Yes, they are. They've helped more people in this town than anyone knows. I've learned much from them. They don't just talk about their faith. They live it."

Becca thought about his words and agreed with him. Whatever kind of woman Abigail had been at one time, she'd grown into a wonderful, giving, caring Christian woman. Meagan had been right, and Becca was glad. She'd come to think of Abigail as a good friend.

The Wellingtons greeted them warmly when Becca and Luke slipped into the pew beside them.

"Good morning," Abigail whispered. "Isn't it a gorgeous day out? Spring will be here before we know it."

"Next week," Becca whispered back. "I love this time of year."

"So do I, and I've noticed some of our trees are already blooming. Others are just about to. You moved here in the dead of winter, but you'll soon see how lovely Hot Springs really is," Abigail said quietly.

The service started just then, and Becca pulled her attention to it. She already felt at home here. The members had all been so welcoming, and she thoroughly enjoyed listening to Pastor Martin speak. His lessons never failed to touch her heart and make her contemplate how she could be a better Christian. Today was no different. The pastor's sermon was about how studying the Word was the only way to stay true to it. By the time the service was over, Becca was determined to ready her Bible daily. She'd gotten out of the habit since her move, and it was time to get back into God's Word.

Sunday dinner at the Wellingtons' was most enjoyable as always, but Becca was looking forward to the drive Luke had promised her. It had been quite cold when she arrived in January, and most of February was, too. But March was giving way to warmer days, and Becca was anxious to see what the landscape looked like all in bloom.

The Wellingtons had asked several other people over for dinner, so of course they couldn't go with Becca and Luke. However, Abigail had some suggestions on what Luke should show her.

"I'll never forget the drive when Marcus took me through town, past Bathhouse Row, up Central Avenue to Ramble and back down Park. The view was stunning. I'm sure it will be the same now. And of course the national park is always a wonderful place to spend an afternoon. It's really a great place to picnic. We'll have to do that soon."

"Actually, what I need to do is invite you and Marcus over for dinner. Please let me know when you have some free time on your calendar."

"Oh, Becca, we'd love to have dinner with you. I'll look over our schedule, but I think we are free this Friday, unless that is too soon for you."

"No. That would work beautifully."

"I'll telephone and let you know for sure later this evening."

"Wonderful!"

It was only when she and Luke were in the hack he'd borrowed from Marcus that Becca became nervous about the invitation. "What was I thinking, Luke? I mean, Abigail and Marcus have a cook who can make anything and could work anywhere. I can never hope to make anything as good as she does."

"Yes, you can. You make several things just as well now. Your roast chicken is as good as any I've tasted. You could serve scalloped potatoes and green beans or corn. Your biscuits are great. Sometimes a simple meal is much more satisfying than one of many courses."

"You'll be there, won't you?"

"Of course, if you want me. And I'll help in any way you need."

"Thank you, Luke."

The rest of the afternoon was very pleasant. Becca loved riding past Bathhouse Row, with all its magnolia trees lined up outside the buildings.

"You'll love the huge blossoms in the summer. They smell wonderful in the heat of the day. Or will you be going home for the break?"

"I might go visit, but I don't want to lose the apartment, and if this is to be my home now, I think I'll spend most of the break right here. I'm hoping my mother might pay me a visit."

From there, Luke turned onto Fountain Street and up to the park. "This is North Mountain. Although the park is under the jurisdiction of a superintendent, elected officials govern the town."

"I knew Hot Springs was part of the park, but I didn't know how it was governed." It was lovely. Luke pointed out the different drives and walks with seats at different intervals. Horse trails had also been developed for those wishing to ride through the park. Becca spotted violets and purple spiderwort peeking out from under the trees, the hickory and oak just beginning to leaf out, the green of the pines among them standing out against the clear blue sky. Sprays of pink phlox added to the color, making Becca anxious to see the park again in a few weeks and discover what else had bloomed.

The chatter of squirrels mixed with the calls of cardinals and blue jays and the sweet song of a mockingbird. It was wonderful to be outdoors.

"Oh, it's so peaceful and beautiful up here. What a wonderful place."

"It is very nice. I don't take the time to come up here as often as I should. I suppose I take some of what Hot Springs has to offer for granted."

They took several different roads winding up and around, and at the last turnaround, Luke headed the buggy back down the mountain. By the time they came out of the park, the sun was beginning to lower over West Mountain.

"Why don't we stop at the Arlington Hotel for a light supper? Then I can take you up Central on the ride Abigail liked so much."

Becca didn't want the afternoon to end. "That would be very nice. Thank you."

The Arlington Hotel was right at the edge of the park on the corner of Fountain Street and Central Avenue. She'd never been to the hotel before but had heard it was very luxurious and that the dining room was excellent.

On entering, Luke led her through the rotunda, and she couldn't help but be impressed. Its walls were finished with oak, and the chandeliers were beautiful. Easy chairs and sofas were positioned near the fireplace. They practically begged for one to sit and talk.

"The height of the resort season for Hot Springs is from January to June, and some of the hotels will close during the slower season. But the Arlington has always stayed open all year around. This is where Abigail stayed when she first came here. She and Marcus come here on special occasions."

"Really?"

He nodded. "Her father had hired Marcus to watch over her when she came here. Things have changed a lot in the last decade. It wasn't common for a young woman to travel alone then, and he wanted to make sure she was safe." He chuckled. "I'm not sure he meant for them to fall in love."

"But it is a wonderful match."

"Yes, it is. And I think Mr. Connors was very happy with the outcome."

They reached the dining room and were shown to a table in an alcove that looked out onto the avenue. Streetlights were coming on, and it felt cozy and private. The waiter must have assumed they were a couple instead of just very good friends. Becca surprised herself by thinking that she wished he were right.

They looked over the menu, and then Luke suggested the chicken with rice. It would be served with soup, macaroni with tomato sauce, and lemon pie for dessert.

"That sounds good. Although I'm not sure it would qualify as light," Becca said.

"Perhaps not. But it is very good."

And it was. The meal, enhanced by the atmosphere, was one of the most enjoyable she'd ever had. Still, she wouldn't trade evenings out at an elegant hotel with the ones she and Luke spent cooking together, discussing their day. No. She wouldn't trade them at all.

After dinner, they came out of the hotel to find that the night was cooling down. But Luke pulled out a lap robe to place over her for the ride up Central over to Ramble and then back down Park Avenue to Central again. Luke stopped at the top of the hill, and just as Abigail had said, the view was spectacular. Night had fallen, and the lights from downtown twinkled from below while the stars in the sky shone brightly in the evening sky. The moon was big and bright and beautiful.

"It is lovely, isn't it?" she breathed.

"It is. I'm glad Abigail suggested that we take this drive."

"I'll have to thank her."

"So will I."

Luke drove the horse and buggy back to the Wellingtons', and after visiting for a few moments, Marcus drove them back to the apartment building. Luke escorted Becca back to her rooms and unlocked the door before handing the key back to her.

"I want to thank you for a really wonderful day," Becca said.

He shook his head. "It's I who should be thanking you. It has been a very special day for me—one I'll remember always."

He couldn't have said anything that would have touched her more. She looked up at him. "So will I."

"Becca—" Luke bent his head and tipped her chin up. His lips softly grazed hers, but before Becca could respond, the sound of the elevator being summoned from another floor startled them both. Luke quickly straightened up and cleared his throat. "I suppose I should let you go in. You have to be alert to keep up with those young people you teach."

"They do keep me on my toes." But a few more minutes wouldn't have made much difference.

"Good night, Becca. I'll see you tomorrow. Thank you again."

"Good night, Luke." She went inside, shut the door, and locked it, her pulse racing. She leaned against the door and touched lips that still tingled from his kiss. Luke had kissed her. He really had.

❧

The week sped by, and after a hectic day on Friday, Becca found herself hurrying home to put away the chicken she'd just bought. Something had happened that morning that had her a little flustered, and she tried to tell herself it was nothing and put it to the back of her mind when Luke showed up to see if she needed help with anything. She'd asked him to make a mayonnaise to dress the salad she was preparing, and while he was stirring it up, he asked how her day went.

"You seem a little. . .flustered. You aren't nervous about the dinner with the Wellingtons tonight, are you?"

"No. At least I don't think so. I—something happened on

my way to school today that bothered me a little."

Luke stopped stirring and gave her his full attention. "What happened?"

"That man that I can't place. . .the one who looks so familiar to me and wants to rent an apartment here. . ."

"What about him? Has he approached you?"

She shook her head. "No. But he was on the trolley this morning. He was standing at the back when I got on and I—" She shook her head. "It's probably all my imagination, but I felt like he was watching me. I can't explain it. I got the shivers, but the trolley stopped, and when I looked back, he'd gotten off. I'm sure it's nothing, and I don't know why running into him bothers me, but it does."

"If you see him again, you let me know right away."

"I'm sure it's nothing, Luke."

"If it makes you feel uncomfortable, it's something I want to know about."

"Hopefully I won't run into him again. Unless he eventually lives in the building."

"That isn't going to happen, Becca. Not now. Not ever."

A knock sounded on the door, and Becca went to answer it. She sighed. So much for putting it all to the back of her mind. But somehow in telling Luke all about it, her spirits had lightened and she was able to greet the Wellingtons with a smile.

ten

Becca entered the small café and waved to Abigail from across the room. She still wasn't sure why her friend had telephoned and invited her to lunch when they'd just had dinner together the night before. But it really didn't matter; she always enjoyed lunching with Abigail. They hadn't gotten to the point of exchanging confidences yet, but she felt they might one day. Maybe Abigail had heard something from Natalie. They hadn't been able to talk much about her last evening.

"I'm so glad you could join me at the last moment," Abigail said when Becca took the seat across from her. "Marcus had a meeting, and well, I just thought it would be nice to get together with you and thank you again for that delicious meal last night."

"You are very welcome. Thank you for coming. I'd been wanting to have you and Marcus over. I know there is no way I'll ever be able to repay you for all you've done for me—"

"Oh, Becca, we don't want repayment. If anything we—I—am so thankful that you've become my friend after all the pain I caused your sister before I left Eureka Springs."

It was the first time there'd been any mention of the heartache Abigail had caused Meagan, but Becca knew about it. Abigail had wanted her brother-in-law, Nate Brooks, for herself after her sister died, and she'd been manipulative and quite horrid to Meagan in trying to keep Nate from falling in love with her. But he had fallen for Meagan, and—the details always became a bit blurry to Becca because she'd only been ten at the time—it all ended with Abigail leaving town and Meagan and Nate getting married.

Abigail had asked for Meagan and Nate's forgiveness long ago, and they'd given it to her. Meagan had told Becca that Abigail had changed over the years, and that was obvious from the kindness she'd shown Becca. But evidently Abigail still felt bad about the events of the past, and she trusted Becca enough to confide in her now.

"Abigail, all that happened long ago. Meagan and Nate speak quite highly of you. You've been so very good to me, and I consider you a wonderful friend. Please put all of that in the past where it belongs. You know that the Lord wants you to accept that you've been forgiven by Him and by Meagan and Nate?"

"I try to forget it, and of course I know I've been forgiven. For that I am truly blessed. But one thing I've learned is that our actions always have consequences. One of them is that we have to live with the wrong we do. I am thankful that Meagan and Nate have had a happy life and am so blessed that Marcus and I do, too. But I did cause a lot of pain for so many back then, and it is something I can never go back and undo. That's the consequence I must live with."

"I understand." Things in Becca's life that she regretted doing popped up in her memory from time to time. "I think we all must deal with that. But we must remember to do as Paul says—forgetting those things that are behind us and going forward toward the goal. That's not it exactly, but you know what I'm saying."

"I do. Becca, I can't tell you how much it means to have you here. I can see why Natalie loves you so much. And speaking of her, I just received a letter from her this morning. While Nate hasn't come around to her moving here, he has said she can visit whenever she wants, and she's hoping to come for Easter. If not then, she says she's coming for sure in May."

"But that is wonderful. It will be so good to see her again. I do miss my family. But with friends like you, Marcus, and Luke, and our church family, I feel more at home here each day."

"It was very good of you to invite Luke for dinner last night."

"Oh, Luke and I have dinner together often."

"You do?"

Becca decided it was time she did some confiding of her own. "Yes. He's been teaching me to cook."

"Luke?"

Becca chuckled at the expression of surprise on Abigail's face. "Yes. He took pity on me my first day of teaching at Central and made dinner for me. It was then that he found out I didn't know much about cooking, and he offered to teach me. He's been collecting recipes from your cook through the years."

Abigail laughed and shook her head. "Well, of all things! Who would have thought that Luke would be a good cook? I just assumed that he ate out a lot, and I wished he'd come eat with us more often. I'll have to tell Cook that he put all her recipes to good use."

"He certainly has. With his help I began to remember some of what Mama had tried to teach me, and with the help of Fannie Farmer's excellent cookbook, we're both learning even more."

Abigail clapped her hands together and smiled. "I'm glad that you and Luke have become such good friends. Marcus and I think of him as family, and I've often thought he seemed lonely. But now that I think about it, he's been much. . .happier in the last few weeks. I think that it might have started when you came into town."

"Oh, I'm sure that's not the reason." Becca only wished it might be.

"Well, I think it is. And there is not a doubt in my mind that it has been good for him to have you around."

For a moment, Becca wanted to tell Abigail of her growing feelings for Luke, but then she decided against it. If Luke didn't feel the same way, it might put Abigail in an awkward position, and Becca liked the way their friendship was growing. She'd keep her thoughts on Luke to herself for now.

❧

The next week found trees and flowers blooming all over the place. Spring was in evidence everywhere, and Becca felt the change deep inside. Each day had become a new adventure that she looked forward to. The Saturday before Easter, she and Luke went on a picnic and took another drive, this time over to Whittington Avenue to see what progress was being made on the alligator farm and to see the Whittington Amusement Park at the head of the avenue.

The alligator farm looked almost ready from what they could tell. They couldn't see any alligators, but the farm was set to open soon. Plans were underway at the high school for an outing later in the spring.

They walked around the outside of the amusement part, which hadn't opened for the season yet, and as Luke talked about all the amusements it offered, Becca found herself looking forward to its opening.

"The park has a summer theater and a music stand, along with a bicycle track, a baseball park, and even a new electric merry-go-round," Luke explained. "In the summer this is a very busy place. They also have concerts twice a week. We'll come over and see a play or listen to the band when it opens for the season, if you'd like."

Luke's smile had her stomach feeling as if a hundred butterflies had just been released inside, and Becca couldn't think of anything she'd rather do than spend a day here with him. "That would be very nice."

Becca's heart felt lighter than it had in a long time, and she was looking forward to the next day. She and Luke were going to the Wellingtons' for a potluck Easter dinner, and she was taking a coconut cake she'd finally perfected. Luke had declared it better than Abigail's cook's. Becca had tasted that cake, and he was giving her high praise indeed.

❧

Becca's sister had sent her a new dress for Easter. It had arrived just the day before, but Becca hadn't opened the package until she had returned home from picnicking and sightseeing with Luke. When she'd unwrapped it, Becca thought it was the most beautiful dress she'd ever seen. It was pink linen trimmed in white, and Natalie had sent a hat to match. Now as she turned this way and that in front of the mirror, Becca was sure it was the prettiest dress she'd ever had.

Instead of Luke meeting Becca in the lobby, he came to get her so that he could carry the basket she'd placed the cake in. As they walked out of the building to the buggy he'd rented from the livery down the street, Becca was in high spirits. Although it was still cool this time of day, the sky was cloudless and the sun shone bright, promising a warm and beautiful day.

Luke put the cake under the seat, securing it so that it wouldn't get jostled on the way to church. She much preferred riding in the buggy on Sundays. He'd been renting one ever since their first ride to the national park, and she and Luke had begun taking an afternoon drive each Sunday after they left the Wellingtons'. She especially enjoyed having a light supper with him at one of the hotels before going home.

Becca knew she'd come to count on Luke more than she should. . .come to care for him too much. But now she couldn't imagine going a whole day without seeing him.

They got to church just as the Wellingtons drove up, and after Luke helped her down, she turned to find Marcus helping someone besides Abigail down from his buggy. She began to smile as she hurried over. Natalie had come for Easter.

The two friends hugged, and Natalie exclaimed, "Oh, Becca! It is so good to see you."

"I was hoping you were coming. Over lunch the other day, Abigail and I were talking about when you might visit." Becca patted the lovely hat Natalie had made her. "Thank you for this beautiful creation. When did you get in town?"

"You're welcome. I arrived early yesterday," Natalie said. "I didn't call because I wanted to surprise you. So Aunt Abigail had the package delivered to you. Becca, Eureka Springs is just not the same place without you, and I've missed you so."

"I've missed you, too."

Natalie looked behind them at Luke, who was talking with Abigail and Marcus. "Not too much, I'm sure. I hear you and Luke have been keeping company."

For a moment Becca was taken aback that Abigail had told her, but when she looked back and saw the older woman shrug and mouth *I'm sorry*, she couldn't be angry. She knew how persistent Natalie could be when she wanted to know something. She smiled at Abigail to show her there were no hard feelings and linked her arm with Natalie's as they headed inside the church. It was wonderful to have her here, and she couldn't wait to hear news from home.

The church service was one she'd remember for a very long time. Pastor Martin made Jesus' death, burial, and resurrection come alive for Becca, and from the sniffling around her, she knew she wasn't the only one who needed the reminder of all that had been sacrificed for her salvation. She prayed that she would keep the memory close to her and not have to be reminded. . .but that she would think upon it each and every day.

The potluck dinner at the Wellingtons' was held outside, where tables had been set up in the backyard, under the oak trees that had leafed out over the past few days. The temperature was just right, not too cool nor too hot, and Becca enjoyed compliments on her cake from all of those around her.

It wasn't until after the surplus of food had been put away that Becca and Natalie got to talk about home.

"How are Mama, Meagan, Sarah, and all my family doing?"

"They are fine. Sarah just glows. She's very happy. But they miss you terribly—almost as much as I do. Well, maybe the same. They are hoping you'll come home for a few weeks this summer. Or perhaps they'll try to come here." Natalie leaned close and whispered, "If I can convince Papa to let me make the move, I'm sure they'll come often."

"Are you making any progress on that front?"

"Maybe a little. I was hoping you might write Mama and see if you could have her talk to Papa. I mean, she is your sister, after all, and you could assure her that you would watch out for me, couldn't you?"

"I suppose I could try."

"Oh, thank you, Becca."

"I can't promise the outcome, though."

"I know. Just try, please."

"All right, I will." It would be good to have Natalie living in the same town.

❧

Luke and Marcus concluded their meeting at the Wellington Agency, and Luke headed back toward the Wellington Building. The assignment he was going on was one he knew he could carry out. He was being sent to Little Rock to track down a suspect in the robbery of one of the Wellington Agency's best clients. Neither Marcus nor the client wanted the police called in unless—or until—their suspicions proved true.

While Marcus had filled Luke in on what he wanted him to do, all Luke could think about was that he didn't want to go, and he'd never felt that way about an assignment before. But he owed Marcus so much; there was no way he was going to try to get out of it. He just wished he didn't have to leave right now.

As he neared the building, he recognized Becca coming from the other direction, and he suddenly knew why he didn't want to go. He didn't want to leave her.

"Good afternoon, Becca. Where have you been?"

"Oh, I had a wonderful lunch with Abigail and Natalie,

and then I went to the grocer's to pick up a few things. I thought I might make a beef stew tonight. Want to join me?"

"Becca, I won't be here this evening. I'm sorry."

"Oh, why, that's all right. I shouldn't have assumed—"

He liked that she had and hurried to reassure her. "No, I'm glad you did. It's just that I'm leaving on the evening train for Little Rock."

"Little Rock? But why?"

"Marcus is sending me on an assignment."

She shook her head. "Assignment?"

"Look, let me help you with your bags, and I'll explain when we get upstairs."

Becca released her grip on one of the bags and kept the lightest one as they went into the building. Mrs. Gentry was just getting on the elevator, and she greeted them cordially.

She smiled at Becca. "Isn't Mr. Monroe a good landlord? He's always willing to help carry up packages or deliver messages. I have a friend in another building, and she says their apartment manager barely speaks to them."

"Oh, that's a shame," Becca replied.

"It is indeed."

"Well, I must tell you that I'll be out of town for a while. But Mr. Easton will be filling in for me."

"Mr. Easton?" Becca asked.

"Yes, he's Marcus's assistant, and he fills in for me when I have to be out of town. We've found it works better than having a full-time assistant manager here."

"He's a very nice man, too," Mrs. Gentry said. "But we will miss you, Mr. Monroe."

It wasn't until they entered Becca's kitchen and put the bags down that she turned to Luke and asked, "Are you going out of town on business for the apartments?"

"No, of course not. I'm on assignment for the Wellington Agency."

"You—you're an agent? An investigator?"

"Why yes. I thought you knew that."

"How would I have known? Oh, I knew you worked for Marcus—I mean, you manage the building for him. But I didn't know that you were an investigator. You never talked about it—never once mentioned it." Becca's voice was low and measured.

She was upset; there was no question about it. But Luke didn't understand why she would be so distressed that he worked for the Wellington Agency. She knew what Marcus did for a living. He shrugged and shook his head. "I thought you knew by now that I was one of the Wellington agents, Becca. I wasn't trying to keep that from you. It just isn't something I normally talk about. But why does it bother you so?"

"It's a dangerous job."

"It can be. But I've been doing it for a long time, and I stand here before you—"

"I lost my fiancé just over a year ago," she said, as if she hadn't heard what he'd said. "He was killed in a bank robbery."

The pain in her eyes was real, and his heart went out to her. "I am truly sorry about your loss, Becca. I wish I'd known. I knew you'd gone through some kind of heartbreak, but I didn't know how to ask you about it. We don't have to talk about it now if you don't want to."

"No. It's all right. In a way, it's good to be able to talk about it. At home my family treats me with kid gloves, as if they are afraid to mention Richard's name to me. I'm not sure that helped me. That is why I moved here—I had to get away from the memories." She took a deep breath before continuing. "Richard was a policeman in Eureka Springs. I'd gone to the bank with a deposit for my sister. I was unaware that it was being robbed until I saw the man turn away from the teller window, a gun in one hand and a bag of money in the other. Before he got to the door, it opened, and Richard burst in. But the robber shot him before he had a chance to. . ." Her voice dwindled off.

Luke waited.

Becca sighed and shook her head. "Richard died in my arms."

Luke released a large breath. "Becca, I am so sorry. That had to be devastating."

Becca began to cry, and he pulled her into his arms. He had to try to comfort her. Someway, somehow. He rocked her back and forth. But he could tell she was still crying. He leaned back and tipped her face up. Her tear-filled eyes broke his heart, and he couldn't keep himself from leaning nearer and capturing her lips with his. When she responded, he deepened the kiss and began to hope that she might return his growing feelings for her.

But then she pushed him way. "No! I never wanted to fall in love with anyone who would willingly put his life on the line in his profession. Not a policeman, not a fireman, not a soldier—no one who puts himself in danger. I promised myself I wouldn't. I don't think I could take the fear of going through that kind of loss ever again, Luke."

Her eyes were swimming in tears, and Luke didn't know what to say next. He certainly couldn't blame Becca for feeling the way she did. Most likely he'd feel the same way had someone he loved died in his arms. No, he couldn't blame her. But he wished she didn't feel that way. With all his heart he wished it.

"I'm so sorry, Becca. I wish I'd mentioned earlier that I also worked as an investigator for the Wellington Agency, but with your connections to the Wellington family, I truly thought you knew. It wasn't something I tried to hide." But he was aware that most people in town thought that he just managed the Wellington Building for Marcus. And that was the way Marcus wanted it. Now that he thought about it, it was probably the reason Becca didn't know.

"Once I proved myself to Marcus, I was promoted to handle some of the harder cases that usually take me out of town. I'm not sent on a regular basis, but when Marcus asks me to take an assignment, I know he wants someone he can depend on to get the job done." Luke made himself stop talking. By the closed look on her face, he figured he was making things worse.

From the way she'd responded to his kiss, he felt she cared about him. But he also knew that being an agent for the Wellington Agency fell into the category of all the things Becca had just said she wanted nothing to do with. All he could do was pray that the Lord would help her change her mind.

There seemed to be nothing left to do but take his leave and say, "I'm sorry. I'll. . .ah. . .I'll see you when I return."

When he got to the door, he turned back to see her wiping her eyes. "I will be back, Becca. That you can count on."

eleven

Luke threw his things in a valise, his desire to leave town totally gone. All he wanted to do was go back to Becca and make sure she was all right. But he couldn't let Marcus down—he owed the man his life. He'd never felt so torn in his life.

He took his case down to the office and waited until Easton showed up. Most likely the watchmen could handle anything that came up, but he felt better knowing someone else was on the premises or nearby. Easton lived down the block and could get there in a matter of minutes if anything happened in the middle of the night.

Luke had never worried overly much when he left, but that was before he'd been asked to watch over Becca Snow and before he'd fallen in love with her. He just wanted her to be safe. He suddenly remembered Becca telling him about seeing Burrows again, and he wondered if he could be the man George had seen several times. He didn't want to leave town without alerting Easton and Marcus to the situation. After putting through a telephone call to Marcus and being assured that a man would be stationed across the street around the clock, he felt better about leaving. But only marginally.

Once he was on the train to Little Rock, Luke tried to think positively. Maybe this was a good thing: to put some space between them. As upset as she was at him and given her reasoning, he hoped that what he felt for her was simply because they'd been spending so much time together. Maybe being away would show him that he didn't care as much as he thought he did. Yeah. And maybe he'd wake up in a different city and forget the kiss they'd just shared. She might say she didn't want to fall in love with—no. She had used the word *wanted*. She said, "I never *wanted*." Not *I didn't want*, or *I don't want*. Not *I never want*, but "I never *wanted* to fall in love." Those were the words she used. Could she possibly have meant that she had already fallen in love? Or was he just grasping at thin air?

★

The first day Luke was gone, Becca tried to tell herself that she was angry with Luke for not telling her that he was a Wellington agent. The next day she was mad at herself for not realizing what should have been obvious. The day after that she just wanted Luke to come back. She missed him more than she wanted to admit, and she worried about him even more. She prayed night and day for him to come home safely.

She'd never felt so torn in her life. She did not want to care that much about the man, but she couldn't get him or his kiss out of her mind. And it didn't help that everywhere she looked she could see him—in the kitchen, where they'd prepared so many dishes, and at the table by the bay window, where they'd eaten those meals. In the elevator, in the lobby, on her way out of the building each morning, and on her way in each afternoon—everywhere she went—she found herself looking for him and then getting angry with herself for caring.

She asked Natalie over for dinner because she just couldn't

sit at the same table by the bay window without missing Luke even more.

"This is delicious, Becca. You did learn to cook."

"Yes, finally. I'm glad you like it." Then, because she felt she should be honest, she added, "Luke taught me a lot."

"Luke did?"

"Yes. Seems he'd been gathering recipes from your aunt's cook for a long time. He really is very good at it."

"Mmm. And so the two of you have been cooking together a lot?"

"Often, yes."

"Isn't he out of town on an assignment for Marcus?"

"Yes." Becca got up to clear the table and bring in dessert.

"May I help?"

"No. I'll be right back." She didn't want Natalie to see the tears that had sprung to her eyes. She cut the chocolate cake she'd made the day before and put the thick slices on dessert plates.

She'd no more than set them down when she sighed. "Oh, I forgot the coffee. I'll be—"

"I'll get the coffee, Becca. You sit down. I didn't come over tonight to have you wait on me. You worked all day."

Becca didn't argue—there would have been no point. Natalie was already in the kitchen. Instead, she dropped down into her chair and looked out on the street. Even with Natalie's company, which she always enjoyed, she was lonesome.

Natalie brought the coffee to the table and poured them both a cup before taking her own seat—or rather, Luke's seat. "Becca, you seem a little on edge tonight. Is something wrong?"

"No, not really. I'm sorry. I just. . .I didn't realize that Luke worked for the Wellington Agency. I thought he just managed this building for Marcus."

"Oh. I can see how that would. . .unsettle you, especially if you didn't know."

"It shouldn't. What he does for a living is really none of my business."

"But of course you care; you've become good friends, Becca. I guess we've all known about Luke's job for so long it never occurred to us to explain."

"There was no reason you should have. Not really. It just surprised me."

"It's more than that. It is really upsetting you."

Memories flashed before Becca, swift and clear, of the night he'd put out the fire, of him bringing supper to her, teaching her how to cook, taking her sightseeing, and. . .the kiss that she couldn't seem to get out of her mind.

"Becca? Have you fallen in love with Luke?"

She looked at her stepniece and best friend. "Oh, I hope not."

"He's a good man, Becca. He would make a wonderful husband."

Becca found herself shaking her head. "I know he's a wonderful person, Natalie. But what he does can be dangerous, and I. . ." Becca sighed and shook her head. "I can't let myself fall in love with him, Natalie. I just can't."

But deep down she was afraid she was very close to doing just that. She had to get over it. Time apart would be good for her. She had to find a way to distance herself from him. What he did was, or could be, as dangerous as Richard's profession. She didn't even know what kind of assignment he'd gone on. . .because she'd gotten too angry to ask. Still, she found herself sending up a silent prayer. *Dear Lord, please keep him safe, whatever he's doing and wherever he is. Please watch over him and bring him back soon. In Jesus' name, I pray. Amen.*

❧

After Becca's dinner with Natalie, the Wellingtons took pity on her and had her over for dinner for the next two evenings. She wondered when Luke would be coming home, but it wasn't something she felt comfortable asking Marcus, so she just waited and worried in quiet.

But she could have hugged Abigail when she asked, "Marcus, have you heard from Luke lately?"

"I had a telegram from him today. Just that he was near to completing his assignment and expected to be back next week."

Since this was Friday, Becca's spirits lifted with the news that he could be home as soon as Sunday. She might want to distance herself from him, but that was emotionally. She wanted to see him back home and know that he was all right. . . and the sooner the better.

Becca was thankful that when she returned from the Wellingtons', she had her work and that it was midterm and she had tests to grade that week. At least that kept her busy for the evening after she got home.

On Saturday she went to lunch with Abigail and Natalie, and they arranged to pick her up for church the next morning. She was grateful for the ride, but coming down to the lobby with no Luke there to greet her left Becca feeling more lonesome than ever.

She did manage to enjoy the afternoon at the Wellingtons' even though it had begun to rain while they were in church. She and Natalie spent the afternoon sipping tea and talking.

Becca listened as Natalie told her about her dreams to open a hat shop in Hot Springs—and that she thought she was close to talking her papa into agreeing to let her try it.

"With Aunt Abby here and now you, too, he's finding it harder to find reasons why I shouldn't move. And he knows I'm not happy in Eureka Springs. Many of my friends have married and moved away. I just don't feel I belong there anymore. I want a change."

"What is it you two are talking about?" Abigail asked as she swept into the room.

"My moving here."

"Oh, I like that subject, don't you, Becca?"

"I do."

"You seem a little down today, dear; is anything wrong?"

For a moment Becca thought Abigail was talking to Natalie until the younger woman said, "She's missing Luke, Aunt Abby."

"Natalie!"

"Well, you've been moping around for days now. I think you—"

"Natalie, dear, if Becca doesn't want to talk about it, then we shouldn't bring it up."

"It's all right, Abigail. It's just that I. . .well. . .I. . ." She didn't know what to say next. She did miss Luke. Much as she tried not to, she did. More with each passing day.

"If you want to talk about it, we are here for you. Anytime. I just don't want you to feel you have to. And as for missing Luke, I miss him, too. It's about time he got back."

"She doesn't want to miss him, Aunt Abby. That's part of the problem."

"Oh?"

"Natalie, you've said quite enough now. I'll tell Abigail the rest."

"Yes, ma'am," Natalie said. But Becca saw the smug smile she tried to hide and realized that Natalie had just accomplished precisely what she had set out to do.

"I think I may have come to care for Luke more than I should. . .and I didn't realize he was also an investigating agent for the Wellington Agency until the day he left. I suppose I should have, but I didn't."

"Oh, my dear. No, there is no reason why you should have. And I am so sorry we didn't make it known to you. But Becca, why would Luke working as an agent distress you so?"

"When I lost Richard, I promised myself that I would never fall in love with anyone who put himself in danger willingly. But I—I just don't know what to do. I want Luke to come home safe, but I feel I must distance myself from him. I just don't think I can take the worry and the fear of going through all that heartache all over again."

Abigail sank down on the couch beside her and hugged her. "Oh, Becca, I do understand. It would be devastating to lose someone else you love. I believe that is a normal reaction to what you've been through. But I also know that no matter how much we might deny our true feelings, the heart doesn't lie. I know you haven't asked, but the best advice I can give you is to take it to the Lord and ask Him to help you to know what to do. And be assured that He does have a plan for you."

❧

Luke had never struggled with an assignment the way he had with this one. Thoughts of Becca were never far away. He tried hard to keep them at bay while he was working. But the desire to get back home spurred him into concentrating on the job at hand. From the leads Marcus had given him and the contacts he'd made from those, Luke found out that the man, whose real name was Charles Williford, lived a double life. Here in Little Rock, he was married with a wife and two children, and from all accounts he was an upstanding citizen and good neighbor.

He worked as a newspaper reporter for the *Arkansas Democrat-Gazette*, where he covered the social life of the Little Rock wealthy. It was also how he found out where and when the rich of that city would be going to Hot Springs or other resorts in the state. But he also pretended to be a businessman from up North, who came to Hot Springs for an occasional weekend for the health benefits of the baths.

Williford would find out which of Little Rock's wealthy families were staying in Hot Springs over a weekend or two, and he would make a trip there himself. But he was careful to come back so that he would be at work when, the next Monday, reports came in from Hot Springs that one of Little Rock's elite had been robbed while on vacation.

Luke had wired Marcus and gotten the orders to tell the police in Little Rock what he'd found out. After a meeting with the chief of police, Luke had agreed to help capture the man.

Now, as he walked into the newsroom and asked a lady he thought might be the receptionist where to find Mr. Williford, policemen stood at every entrance and exit of the building.

The young woman pointed to a row of desks. "His desk is about midway down the aisle. You can go on back."

"Thank you," Luke said. As he walked through the room, he checked to see where the closest exit was. It was near the back and had a frosted-glass window in the door. He was pretty sure the shadow he saw was of uniformed police—at least he hoped so, because experience told him that Mr. Williford would take off as soon as he realized what Luke was questioning him about.

The man's head was bent over his Underwood typewriter, and his fingers were tapping away. He was larger than Luke had expected. Luke cleared his throat, trying to get the man's attention, but he kept right on typing. "Mr. Williford, may I have a word with you?"

"Be with you in a minute," he said without looking up. "Take a seat."

Luke did just that. He sat looking at the burly man and wondering why he would have turned to a life of crime when he had a good job and—

"What can I do for you? Got a social event you want to put in the paper?"

"No. I just came to ask you a question or two. I've been told you might know someone I'm looking for."

"Oh? Who is that? And who are you?"

"My name is Luke Monroe. The man I'm looking for goes by the name of Gibson. Dub Gibson." Luke watched the color drain from the man's face, telling him what he needed to know.

But old Charley kept his composure; Luke would give him that. The man shook his head. "Nope. Never heard of him."

"Are you sure? The desk clerk at the Hale House in Hot Springs says he was given your name as a contact in case he ever had any juicy stories about the hotel's clientele. Gibson told him you'd pay well for a good story."

"Well, maybe I did business with someone he knew, but

like I said, I don't know anyone by the name of Gibson."

"Oh, I think you do. In fact—"

"Mr. Monroe, I've told you I don't know him. I've got work to do. Now kindly leave before I call the security guard."

Luke stood. "Why don't you call him on over? I'm sure he'll be interested to know what the Wellington Agency has to say about Mr. Gibson and you."

The man pushed back his chair and stood. He was big, just as Luke had thought. And tall. He had at least four inches on Luke, who was close to six feet, and probably weighed fifty pounds more. "I just want to talk to you, Gibson."

"Well, I don't want to talk to you."

Luke let the man's words sink in. It sounded like Williford had just admitted he was Gibson. "Got something to hide?"

"Why, you little pip-squeak. . ."

Williford came toward Luke like an enraged mama bear. Luke stood his ground. "You aren't going to get away with it, you know."

"Elliot," Williford bellowed. "Get this man out of here, or I will."

Evidently Elliot was a guard, and he was standing up by the door Luke had come in through. He headed their way but not before he knocked on the door.

"What is it, Mr. Williford?" The front door opened, and two policemen burst into the room.

"Why, you little traitor!" Williford yelled at the guard. He grabbed Luke's shoulder.

Before Luke could throw a punch, Williford threw a blow

at him that had him seeing stars, then he knocked Luke out of
the way, sending him flying across one desk and plowing into
the corner of the next one. Luke's head felt as if a starburst
had gone off inside, but he didn't have time to think about it
as he pulled himself up and got his bearings. He felt a little
light-headed, but he had to see this through. Williford was
headed for the back exit closest to his desk. Luke followed.

"Stop, or we'll shoot," one of the cops behind him yelled
before he passed Luke. Luke came up in the rear as they
moved closer to Williford. The man was almost at the door.
He yanked it open and ran right into the two policemen
waiting for him. He was handcuffed in a matter of seconds
and taken into custody.

His hate-filled eyes met Luke's gaze. If looks could kill,
Luke knew he'd be dead.

"Mr. Monroe, sir," one of the policemen said.

"Yes?" Luke was feeling a bit nauseated.

"I think we better get you to a doctor."

"Why?"

"Sir, your head is bleeding."

Luke reached up and felt the wetness. He brought his
hand down and saw that, indeed, his head was bleeding.
But that wasn't the only place that was hurting. He'd hit his
right shoulder on the corner of the desk, and he had no
doubt that it would be giving him trouble for some time to
come. "I think you are right."

"I'll take you. Then we'll go back to the police station. I
think you can add some charges of your own to the long list
Williford already has."

Luke nodded and found it hurt to do even that. He felt a
little sick as he looked at his arm. His arm would heal, and

he'd be all right. The job he'd been sent to do was almost done. But most important was that he'd get to go home very soon. "I think I can add some charges. Let's go."

twelve

Burrows followed the woman to the post office. It had become imperative that he find out if she remembered him. His future here could be at stake. This was his home, and he'd felt safe here for the past two years. He'd never liked robbing banks in the places he lived. He liked living here. His wife was happy, and it made a good base from where to work. He didn't want to have to move away. He thought he knew who this woman was. He'd done some digging in his files after he saw her when he was leaving the Wellington Building that day.

The newspaper photograph was grainy, but he was almost positive that it was her. The picture had been taken right after the robbery at a bank in Eureka Springs more than a year ago. In her arms she was holding the policeman he'd killed. The caption said her name was Rebecca Snow and she was a teacher. It all made sense; he'd followed her to the high school, so this woman must also be a teacher. But still, the young woman here could just look like the one in the paper. The hairstyles were different, and in the picture he couldn't see her eyes because she was looking at the man in her arms.

Yet he couldn't be totally sure. Just because he thought she was the same woman didn't mean that she was. He watched her go inside the post office. Now was the time to find out. He stepped into the building. She'd approached the postmaster and waited for him to get her mail, then she handed him several letters and turned to leave. Their eyes met before he could turn away.

She got to him and stopped. His heart dropped. Did she know?

"Excuse me, sir. You seem very familiar to me, but I can't place you. I—"

"Sorry, miss. I've never met you before." He tried to stay calm and moved past her to buy some stamps. He could only hope that she left. His heart thudded as he turned to leave. She was gone. He breathed a sigh of relief before he rushed out of the post office. He could see her a block away, and he turned in the opposite direction. If she was the same woman—and he was almost certain she was—it would only be a matter of time before she remembered just where she had seen him. It was time to make a trip to Eureka Springs and see if Miss Rebecca Snow still lived there. His steps quickened as he headed to the train depot. He'd take the next train out.

❧

All the way down to the Arlington Hotel, where she was meeting Natalie and Abigail for lunch, Becca tried to place where she'd seen the man she seemed to run into on a fairly regular basis. She pretty much went to the same places—the grocer, the post office, the bookstore, school, church, and of course, the Wellingtons'. Probably she'd passed him on the street going to one or the other of those places, and that was why he'd looked so familiar to her when she'd bumped into him at the grocer's that day.

But while that reasoning made sense to her, she could not get rid of the feeling that she'd seen him before she arrived in Hot Springs. Something about the man just sent shivers down her spine, and she didn't know why when she didn't even know who he was. Becca sighed and shook her head. What did it all matter anyway—other than to keep her mind off Luke?

Becca knew what she was doing. She was trying to occupy her thoughts with anything or anyone besides Luke. She missed him more with each passing day, and it was nearly impossible to keep from thinking about him.

She reached the Arlington and was glad to find that Natalie and Abigail were there ahead of her. With Luke gone, she didn't look forward to much except being at school and spending time with her two best friends.

"We were getting worried about you," Abigail said when Becca was seated across from her.

"What took you so long?" Natalie asked.

"I had to run to the post office to mail some letters home."

Her nights were the loneliest without Luke around. She'd reverted to having a very light supper, after which she pored over her cookbook or caught up on her letter writing to her mother and sisters. She'd just received one from her mother the day before. "Remember you asked me to write Meagan? And Mama is talking about coming for a visit—I'm trying to convince her to do that. I wish she would. I do miss her."

"What is the news from home? Anything exciting? I haven't heard from Mama and Papa since last week."

Becca tore into her letter and skimmed it for news she could report. "Everyone is doing fine, according to Mama. She says Sarah is growing larger each day, and they've wondered if she might have twins. They run in Mitch's family, you know."

"Oh, that would be something, wouldn't it?" Natalie asked.

"Mama says there is a new minister in town, Natalie. Why

didn't you tell us about him?"

The younger woman shrugged. "I didn't know you'd be interested. He's young."

"Mmm. Mama says he is very nice looking, too. And that he seemed quite interested in you." Becca was sure Natalie blushed at her words. "She thinks he may be the reason you came back to Hot Springs."

"Why, I came back to see you and Aunt Abigail. I. . .he. . ." Natalie stopped and shrugged again. "He would like to court me. I'm just not sure how I feel about that. I mean, I don't think I am meant to be a minister's wife, but he. . .well, he is a very good man and. . ." She sighed. "I'm hoping the Lord will help me decide what to do."

"That is the best thing you can do, dear," Abigail said, looking from Natalie to Becca. "The Lord has someone in mind for each of you. I know from experience it is much better to let Him bring two people together than to try to make something happen. Much better." She took a sip of tea and smiled before adding, "I think you'd make a very good minister's wife, Natalie dear."

Becca felt that Abigail had been talking about herself and Marcus and also about Meagan and Nate. And while her friend's advice was good, Becca knew firsthand how hard it was not to want to control one's heart. She didn't want to care so much about Luke, but she was getting nowhere telling herself not to care. She could fight her feelings all she wanted, but that didn't stop her from thinking about him. And it didn't keep memories of his kiss at bay.

Were these thoughts and feelings God's will for her and Luke? She didn't know. And if he didn't come home soon, how was she ever going to find out?

"Becca?" Natalie brought her out of her thoughts. "Did you hear what Aunt Abby said?"

"I'm sorry. I must have been woolgathering. What did you say, Abigail?"

"I was saying that I believe Luke will be home soon. Marcus had a telegram from him, and he was quite pleased with Luke's work."

Becca's heart did a little somersault before righting itself in her chest. Luke was coming home. "Did he say when he'd be coming back?"

"No. And the telephone rang just then, and I forgot to ask. I'm sorry."

"Oh no. There is nothing to be sorry about." Luke would be home soon, and that was what mattered. Had she not come to lunch today, she might not have known. Just the knowledge that she would see him before long and that he was all right made the day brighter and her mood much lighter.

☙

After lunch Becca, Natalie, and Abigail did some shopping, and by the time they parted company, Becca was in much better spirits. Perhaps Luke would be home tomorrow or at the very least by Monday. She didn't know how she would react when he saw him. She only knew that she wanted him back here at the Wellington Building, helping her to cook, being in her life. . .as the person who'd become her very best friend.

That she felt more for him than that, she tried not to think about. And she tried not to dwell on what his kiss meant about the way he felt. All she really knew was that she missed him and couldn't wait to see him again.

"Good afternoon, Miss Snow," George said as she entered the building.

"Good afternoon. It's a beautiful day out," Becca said. She wanted to ask if Luke was back, but one look at his office showed that he wasn't. As she headed toward the elevator and glanced into the office, it was Mr. Easton she saw. She gave him a wave and stepped onto the elevator.

There was no way to know what train Luke took out of Little Rock, and he might not be on one yet. There was nothing to do but wait. . .and pray that they were still friends when he got back.

She met up with Mrs. Gentry in the hall. "Good day, Mrs. Gentry. How are you doing?"

"I'm fine, dear. I'd be better if Mr. Monroe would get back in town."

"Oh, do you need something? Can I help? Or I'm sure Mr. Easton would."

"I don't need anything. I just miss seeing Mr. Monroe. He's always so kind, and he checks on me. I haven't seen Mr. Easton checking on anyone since Luke went away. I don't like it when Luke goes out of town. It's just lonely without him around."

Becca felt exactly the same way. "It will be good to have him back."

"Yes, it will. I'm on my way down to the Townsends'. I told them I would watch their children tonight. It's their anniversary, and they are going to dinner at the Arlington."

"That's very nice of you."

"It's nice of *them*. It gives me something to do besides crochet. These hands get a little stiff if I keep at it too long." The older woman waved and went on her way, leaving Becca to think how selfish she'd been. Instead of feeling sorry for herself because she didn't have Luke to share a meal with, she could have invited Mrs. Gentry over, and they'd both have been a bit less lonely. She might be new in town, but Mrs. Gentry was a widow without any family around from what Becca could tell. She was ashamed that she hadn't made more of an effort to get to know her neighbors and promised herself that she would do better from now on. She'd spent too much time moping around her apartment with Luke gone and more than enough time thinking about a man she only wanted as a friend.

Disgusted with herself, Becca put up her purchases and went to fix a light supper. But frying bacon and eggs only served to bring Luke to mind once again. She couldn't help but remember the night she'd nearly set the kitchen on fire and Luke had come to her rescue.

He hadn't ever told a soul about her mishap. Nor had he teased her about it. No. Instead he'd offered to teach her to cook. Becca's heart filled with. . .love? No. She didn't want to love Luke—didn't want to love anyone who put his life in danger as Richard had. She didn't want to live with that fear. . .never again.

She took her supper to the table where she and Luke had shared their meals and looked out onto the street below as she had so many times. But the spot felt even lonelier tonight, so she picked up her plate and headed toward the dining room. But that table was so big, she didn't even sit down. Finally, she made her way back to the small table at the end of the kitchen and sat down to eat. But the eggs were cold, and she'd lost her appetite, so she scraped her plate and washed dishes.

Streetlights were coming on when she went back to the living room. She picked up a book she'd purchased that afternoon, *Kim* by Rudyard Kipling. She'd heard it was an excellent book and had been looking forward to reading it. But hard as she tried to get interested in it, she just could not concentrate. She found herself listening to the normal sounds of the building. She heard the elevator stop on her floor and held her breath, hoping to hear footsteps come her way, signaling that Luke was back, but the footsteps seemed to go in the other direction.

Becca sighed and set the book down. She'd been so confused since Luke left. She truly didn't want to fall in love with him, but she was afraid she was more than halfway there. If it wasn't meant to be, she needed to stop thinking about him. "Dear Father, please help me. I don't know what to do. I know I care too much for Luke, unless it is in Your will that I do. I don't want to. You know why. I'm not sure I can give my heart to someone who chooses to put his life in danger again. I. . .I don't want to lose anyone else I love. Please help me to put Luke out of my mind or show me that it is in Your will for me to care about him. Please let me know what to do. And please let Luke get home safely. In Jesus' name, I pray. Amen."

A knock sounded on the door, and her heart jumped. Could it be Luke? She hurried to answer the door, and what she saw when she opened it made her gasp.

❧

Luke knew he looked bad, but if he'd known Becca would be so shocked, he'd have waited to come see her. Her eyes were huge and sorrowful as they took in his black eye and the bandage on his forehead.

Her hands were over her mouth, but she moved them long enough to say, "What happened to you?"

"It isn't as bad as it looks," Luke said. "I promise."

She didn't seem convinced. "Who did that to you? What happened, Luke?"

"May I come in?"

"Of course." Becca stepped back, but her eyes never left his face. Good thing she couldn't see his shoulder and upper chest where he'd hit the desk.

She motioned for him to take a seat in the chair by the fireplace, and she took a seat on the footstool in front of him. "Did you have to have stitches?"

"A few. I'm fine, Becca, really. If it makes you feel any better, the bad guy is in jail."

"I would hope so. Are you going to tell me what happened?"

There didn't seem to be any way around it, so Luke launched into a detailed account of his assignment. Becca listened intently, but when he got to the part where Williford knocked him across the room, she jumped up and put her hand to her throat, her eyes filling with tears.

"Becca." His voice had her turning away. Luke stood and turned her toward him. Two teardrops slid down her cheeks as she looked into his eyes. "Becca, I am all right. I'm right here with you. I came back, just as I said I would."

She began to sob, and Luke pulled her into his arms. He tipped her face up and bent his own until their lips met. The taste of salty tears was on her lips as she kissed him back before quickly pulling away and brushing at her tears. But she'd responded just enough so that finally, in his heart, Luke knew that Becca cared for him, too.

That knowledge brought its own set of problems. She

knew he was an agent for Marcus, and she didn't like it one bit. Yet she didn't know about his past, and he couldn't bring himself to tell her now. For once he did, he feared the two of them would have no future.

thirteen

Burrows had been in Eureka Springs for just over a week before he had his answers. He'd watched the Snow home every day, but he'd never seen anyone come out who looked like the woman in the picture.

Finally, he'd gone to the high school and pretended to be a parent who was checking out the education system in Eureka Springs before making a move to the city. The principal, Mr. Johnson, had been very nice and had taken him around the school, introducing him to many teachers, but there hadn't been one named Snow, nor was there anyone who looked like her teaching there.

As he got ready to leave, he finally learned all he needed to know.

"I thank you, sir, for showing me around."

"You are welcome, Mr. Burrows. I can assure you that we have an excellent staff and student body here. Your child—did you say it was your daughter or son who'd be attending?"

"Ah. . .I have both," Burrows lied. "A boy and a girl."

"Well, I assure you they will be happy here. I look forward to welcoming them personally. Where is it you said you'd be moving from?"

"Hot Springs, sir. A city not totally unlike your own."

"Ahh. We lost one of our best teachers to your town. A Miss Snow transferred there in the middle of the year. It was certainly our loss and Hot Springs's gain. Perhaps one of your children has her for a teacher."

"Hmm, I don't believe so, but I will ask. I'd best be on my way. Thank you again, Mr. Johnson. You've given me all the information I need."

The two men shook hands, and Burrows walked outside. He felt almost giddy, realizing that he'd found out all he needed to know. How easy this had been. He should have come here right from the first. Now all he had to do was go back home and wait for the opportune moment to take care of Miss Snow.

⁂

Over the next few weeks, Becca and Luke slipped back into their routine of cooking and eating together most evenings. Her world finally felt back to normal. . .although it really wasn't. And while there wasn't another kiss, there was no way to deny that their relationship had undergone a subtle change.

She had no doubt that Luke cared about her, but since the night he'd come home, he seemed a little distant at times. And she went from being elated that Luke was home and seemed to have missed her as much as she missed him, to feeling panic that his profession was one that would take him away fairly often and that he would be no safer than the fiancé she'd lost in the line of duty.

Still, she couldn't stop her heart from turning to mush each time she saw the fading bruise around his eye and on his forehead. He could have been killed in that brawl. Oh why did life have to be so complicated? Why did her feelings for Luke seem to grow with each passing day. . .no matter how hard she tried to keep them at the friendship level?

Every day she prayed for the Lord to show her what to do,

to let her know if she and Luke were meant to be together or not. If not, most likely she needed to find another place to live. She wasn't sure she could stay in the same building, seeing him every day and wanting to be with him more all the time.

Thoughts of Luke were never far away, and this warm first day of May, as she and other teachers took their classes to the newly opened alligator farm as one of their May Day events, was no exception.

The reptiles weren't very appealing to Becca, but her students thought they were quite entertaining. The boys did anyway. The girls still kept their distance as the owner, Mr. Campbell, showed them around. He pointed to a male and female sunning themselves onshore.

"Just don't get too close," he admonished.

Becca knew the girls would heed his advice; it was the boys she worried about as they lagged behind and pushed each other a little closer to the gators.

"It looks like they have armor on," Milly Roberts said. She'd become one of Becca's favorite students and was quick to learn.

"And they are really ugly," Elizabeth Miller added.

Becca chuckled. "I agree completely, girls."

But when Mr. Campbell brought out a hatchling that was only about eight inches long, they all gathered around the man.

"Oh how cute. Perhaps they just get uglier with age," Milly said.

"They do seem to, don't they?" Mr. Campbell agreed. "Perhaps it's because they aren't so dangerous at this age."

"How fast can they move?" Elizabeth asked.

"Across land about eight miles an hour for short distances,

but not as fast if it's more than a few yards, and in water they can go about ten miles an hour."

Suddenly a commotion from the shoreline of the pond caught their attention. As they hurried in that direction, it seemed that one of the boys had climbed over the fenced-in area and had fallen in, and one of the alligators was headed down the embankment to join him. Another boy had found a huge limb somewhere, and several of the boys took hold of one end while holding it out over the boy so they could drag him back up the embankment. Mr. Campbell and one of his assistants ran to help.

Once the boy was onshore, his teacher took control of the situation and headed the group back to the school. Becca breathed a sigh of relief that none of her students had been in danger; it put a damper on the afternoon though, and everyone seemed in one accord to end the excursion.

Becca gathered the students she was in charge of and they started back to school. When they came out of the gate, her heart did a little flip to see Luke standing there. When she'd mentioned the field trip to him the night before, he'd said he might join them, but she figured he was busy.

"Looks like I missed all the excitement." He grinned at Becca. "What happened?"

Luke seemed impervious to the curious glances he was getting from her students, but Becca wasn't. She was sure she'd be asked all kinds of questions about him, so it would be best just to introduce him. "Everyone, this is Mr. Monroe. He is a friend of mine."

She quickly introduced the students around them by first names, and after a chorus of "Pleased to meet you" from everyone, she went on to explain about the boy falling in the pond.

"Wish I'd seen that." Luke chuckled along with the other males in the group.

"It was quite frightening for a few minutes when the big old alligator headed toward him," Jennifer said. "But thankfully, some of the other boys pulled him to safety."

"Yes, well, I guess that would be frightening," Luke agreed. He bent low and whispered to Becca, "I still wish I'd been here to see it."

She smiled and shook her head.

"Well, I guess I'll go back to work. I'll see you later?" he asked, looking into her eyes.

For a moment Becca forgot young people surrounded them as she smiled up at him. "Of course."

Luke tipped his hat and went on his way as Becca and her students made their way back to school.

"He's very handsome, Miss Snow. Is he your beau?" Milly asked.

Was he? Becca didn't know how to answer other than to say, "We're just good friends. I don't have a beau."

"Oh, that's too bad," Elizabeth said. "You look very good together. He seems quite smitten with you."

Becca only knew that she was quite smitten with him.

❧

Luke left Becca and her students, fully aware that they could see he was quite infatuated with their teacher. He couldn't hide how he felt. He was in love with Becca Snow. No doubt about it. She was on his mind every waking moment, and most of his dreams centered on her, too. And from the way she'd responded to his kiss the night he came home and the way she'd looked at him just now, color stealing up her neck and onto her cheeks, he was pretty certain she felt the same way.

But she seemed to be trying hard not to. He was also sure of that. Luke didn't think she could control her heart any more than he could. At least for now. But once she found out about his past, that could be a whole different story, and he knew he had to tell her. He might lose her, but he couldn't live with himself if he didn't tell her the truth.

He got back to the building just as Marcus was walking out.

"Did we have a meeting today? I'm sorry—"

"No. We didn't. I just thought I'd stop by and visit awhile. Why don't we go have coffee at the corner café that just opened down the street? I hear they have really good pie."

"Sounds fine to me." Luke hoped he wasn't about to get another assignment, at least not yet. He couldn't remember ever wishing that until just now, and he knew it had to do with Becca. He didn't want to leave her again, at least not until he knew how she felt about him.

They reached the café and gave their orders for coffee and cherry pie before Luke asked, "How are Abigail and Natalie? Has she decided to open a shop here?"

"She's looked at a few places, but Natalie doesn't really seem to be decided on moving just yet. And she's wondering if Becca might decide to go back to Eureka Springs now that the school year is almost finished."

Luke's heart seemed to stop. *Dear Lord, please don't let that happen.* "Has Becca said anything about it to her?"

Marcus shook his head. "Not that I know of. And from what I can tell, Becca loves teaching here. She mentioned that she hopes some of her family will come for a visit this summer. I'm not sure what Natalie is basing her thinking on. Abigail mentioned that there was a possibility of a romance for her back home."

"Becca?" Luke held his breath, waiting for Marcus's answer.

"No. Natalie."

"Oh." Luke breathed a huge sigh of relief. "Well, I certainly hope she is wrong about Becca moving back home."

"Ahh. It's that way, is it?" Marcus grinned at him.

Luke sighed. He'd spoken without thinking but decided it was time he talked to someone about it; he couldn't think of another person he trusted as much as he did Marcus. He didn't beat around the bush. "I've fallen in love with her."

"I thought that might be the case. She's a wonderful woman, Luke. You couldn't choose anyone whom Abigail and I would be happier for you to fall in love with."

"Now the trick is to find out if she could ever feel the same way."

"You don't know?"

Their pie and coffee arrived just then, and Luke waited until the waitress left the table to answer. "I believe she does. But she doesn't want to."

"Why not?"

"She thinks my work with the agency is as dangerous as her fiancé's was. You knew he'd been shot in a bank robbery, didn't you?"

"I didn't know all the details, but I knew he was a policeman who'd been shot."

Luke nodded and took a sip of coffee. "I suppose it's natural for her not to want to care for someone who could be in danger. But what I do is nothing like being a policeman, fireman, or soldier."

Marcus looked over the coffee cup he'd just brought to his mouth. "I don't suppose those bruises that have just faded gave her much confidence," he said before taking a sip from the cup.

"No. Good thing she never saw the rest of them." Luke forked a piece of pie into his mouth and chewed.

"She hasn't sent you on your way, telling you to leave her alone, has she?"

"Not yet."

"Then all is not lost. Have you told her how you feel?"

"That I love her and want her to be my wife? No."

"Why not?"

"Because when I do—or before I do—I have to tell her about my past."

"Your past? Luke, you were cleared of any wrongdoing."

"I know. But still, I was in prison, and she's such a genteel woman. . . ." He shook his head. "Even if she didn't have a problem with it, her family might."

"Well, I agree she should know. But I don't think it is going to be the problem you perceive it to be."

"Then there is the difference in our ages—"

"I've seen the way she looks at you, Luke. I'm pretty certain your age is not a problem at all. And just so you know, Abigail thinks Becca is in love with you."

Luke's heart swelled with hope, and he silently prayed that Marcus was right on all counts. Then another thought came to him. "What if Natalie is right, and Becca moves back home this summer?"

"I don't think that is going to happen. But if she does, then you'll know she's not ready to risk her heart again. You need to tell her about your past and how you feel about her. Only then will you know how she feels. It is something better found out now rather than later."

"I know. I'll talk to her soon."

"I think you should."

"I'll do it tonight." Luke dreaded it with every fiber of his being, but Marcus was right. He could no longer put it off.

fourteen

By the time Becca got home that afternoon, she was certain that all of her students and most of the teachers thought Luke was courting her—no matter how hard she tried to convince them otherwise.

She thought her students had lots of questions until she went to the teachers' lounge after school.

"Was that your beau, Becca?" Jennifer Collins asked.

"No. He's a good friend though. I'd mentioned that we were going on a field trip today, and he came by."

"You didn't see any young man coming to the alligator farm just because I was there." Lila Baxter gave an exaggerated sigh. "I could only wish to have someone that nice looking spending time with me."

"He is very handsome," Mrs. Richards said. "And I've been around a long time. I know that lovelorn look when I see it."

Becca laughed, but she could feel the color steal up her face as she shook her head and said, "Really, he's just a very good friend."

"Then you need glasses, Becca. The man doesn't want to just be a friend to you. And from what I saw, you care more than that, too," Jennifer said.

Becca couldn't very well deny the truth, so she said nothing. She just gathered her things and shook her head as she left the room.

She'd been praying very hard to know what to do. She

could no longer deny that she cared deeply about Luke. She did. But she was so afraid of losing someone else she loved that she felt paralyzed about what to do.

Still, it didn't keep her pulse from racing when she saw Luke that evening. She told herself it was all the talk about him being her beau and courting her that had her reacting the way she was. She didn't go around thinking in those terms, but now that they'd been brought up, she couldn't seem to get them out of her mind.

Thankfully, he didn't seem to notice how flustered she was as they worked together in her kitchen to prepare supper. They'd made a soup from leftovers from the night before, and he'd brought crusty bread to go along with it.

They talked about the outing and what she thought of the alligator farm.

"If it hadn't ended so abruptly, perhaps I would have enjoyed it, but trying to keep up with students made it a little hard."

"I can see how it would. It's springtime, and young men get a little silly."

"Oh?" Becca looked up to see his gaze on her. A small smile played around his lips.

"Yes."

Something in his expression had her asking, "Why is that?"

"Because their thoughts turn to love."

"Really?" Becca caught her breath at the look in his eyes.

"Really. It happens with grown men, too. Becca, I must tell you something."

Her heart felt as if it had stopped. "All right. Go ahead."

"There are some things you don't know about me. Things I must tell you before. . ."

She nodded and waited.

Luke released a big sigh and stood up. He put his hands in his pockets and looked down at the floor for a moment before sitting back down across from her. "When I was about sixteen, my mother passed away. My papa seemed to lose interest in everything after she died. . .including me."

"I'm so sorry, Luke." Becca's heart went out to the lonely boy he must have been. She reached out and touched his hand.

He put his larger one on top of hers and grasped her fingers. He shrugged and continued. "I was on my own most of the time, and I. . .well. . .I hung around some older boys sometimes. They liked to pull pranks, and when I was with them, I went along. Until the night they wanted to rob a store."

Becca gasped, and Luke got up from the table again. It was obvious that this wasn't getting any easier for him to tell. "I didn't go with them. I told them no and went to my aunt Carrie's, my mother's younger sister. She'd been trying to talk to me, tell me I was in with the wrong crowd. I finally knew she'd been right. Anyway, going to her house turned out to be the best thing I could have done. I knew my papa wouldn't know if I was at home or not. He'd taken to drinking by that time, and well, anyway, I stayed the night with Aunt Carrie and Uncle Jerome and went home the next morning."

Becca breathed a sigh of relief that he'd known where to go. "I didn't know you had an aunt. Does she live here?"

"No. She lives up in Fort Smith. That's where I'm from."

"Oh, I remember you telling me that. What happened then?"

"Nothing for several days. Then the cops showed up and arrested me for the robbery."

"But you weren't even there."

"No. I wasn't. But my so-called friends said I was and that I was the one who did it. Once Aunt Carrie knew what happened, she contacted the police and told them I was at her home that night, but they said it didn't matter; I could have robbed the store before I went to her house. She saw an advertisement in the newspaper about the Wellington Agency when it was just starting out, and she wrote to Marcus and asked him to investigate. She didn't think he'd answer, but he came all the way up there to talk to her. She didn't have much money but gave him what she could and said we'd pay him back as soon as we could."

"Of course Marcus took the case."

"Yes. And to make a very long story short, he found witnesses who saw four boys on the corner that night but saw that one had left earlier—before the store was robbed. That was me. But they beat up the shopkeeper so badly he nearly died. His memory was fuzzy, and he couldn't be certain who attacked him, at first. Thankfully, he finally remembered before it was all over with.

"It took several weeks, but Marcus cleared my name. That alone would have indebted me to him, but then he offered me a job to learn from him and a place to stay—to get away from Fort Smith and start life over here in Hot Springs. But most important of all, he led me to the Lord. I don't think I can ever repay him for all he's done for me."

Becca could certainly see how and why he would feel so beholden to Marcus. "Oh, Luke. I'm so sorry you had to endure all of that and that you had to spend time in prison for something you didn't do."

"But what would your family think?"

"My family?" Becca wasn't sure what he was getting at.

He'd told her so much, and she understood him much better now but...

"Would they ever allow me to court you?"

Becca's heart filled with love for this man. She cared so very much for him...but...

"Becca? You do believe me, don't you?"

"Yes, Luke, of course I believe you. And my family would approve of you; I am sure of that. But I...I..."

Luke stood. "I think I understand. You don't care about me in that way—" He turned to look out the window.

Becca jumped up and went over to him. She reached out and touched his shoulder. "Luke, that is not what I am saying at all. It's just that in the last few weeks, you've revealed things about yourself to me that, well, they are very important, and I can't help but wonder what else you haven't told me about yourself. What else is there about you that I should know?"

❧

Luke looked down into the eyes of the woman he wanted but was afraid he'd never have. "The only thing left that I haven't told you...the only thing that you need to know...is that I love you. With all my heart."

"Luke, I—"

"It's all right, Becca. I know now that there is no chance for us. I think I've known it all along, but I wanted so badly to be wrong. Now that I've told you about my past, I realize that you deserve someone who can offer you so much more than I can. You don't need someone in your life whose past could come back to haunt your future. Even though I was cleared, some people would wonder about it all if they found out I was once in prison. I can't ask you to take that on."

"I'm sorry. I just wanted to know what else—"

"There is no need to be sorry. And there is nothing else to tell. You've endured so much with the death of your fiancé, and I can understand how you would have reservations about my career. But I can't think of another career I would want, and I do feel loyal to Marcus. He taught me all I know, and he counts on me. I wish things were different." He saw the sheen of tears in Becca's eyes, but she didn't say anything. He didn't want her pity. He only wanted her love. It seemed that wasn't to be.

"I will always love you, Becca. But I know I am not right for you. I can only now wish you the very best life has to offer and let you find what that is." With that, Luke walked out of her apartment and down the hall.

Everything in him cried for her to open that door and call him back—for her to tell him she loved him, too. He felt she did. But evidently she still didn't want to, and there was nothing else he could say to change that fact.

He unlocked his door and waited a second. He heard no sound of a door opening, no call to bring him back. He walked in and sat down in his favorite chair. His heart felt as if it were being squeezed and wrung out, and he wasn't sure what to do other than pray. "Dear Lord, please help this pain go away. I knew that my chance to win Becca's heart was not good, and I didn't want to fall in love with her. But I do love her, Lord. Please help me to give up gracefully and be happy for her no matter who she chooses to spend her life with. You've blessed me with more than I ever dared dream, and I thank You for all that You've given me. I just ask that You continue to watch over her as I feel I must try to pull back from spending so much time with her. I value her friendship and would pray that we can still be friends, but please help me to get over the hurt of knowing that's all she feels for me. In Jesus' name, I pray. Amen."

Luke felt only marginally better after praying, but he trusted that the Lord would answer.

He felt bad that he hadn't stayed to help Becca clear the table and clean up the kitchen as he usually did, but he just couldn't stay. Now all he wanted to do was go back. Should he go apologize and help her wash dishes? He stood up and started toward the door. Then he stopped. What was he doing?

His telephone rang just then, and his heart jumped. He strode over and picked up the earpiece from its hook. Maybe it was Becca. Maybe—he spoke into the mouthpiece. "Hello?"

"Luke?"

His heart fell at the sound on the other end of the receiver. "Good evening, Marcus. What can I do for you?"

"We need to talk. I've just had a report from Nelson, and it also concerns Becca. It may be time for you to go on another assignment. Can you come over now?"

Maybe it was just what he needed, to get out of town and away from the heartache he was experiencing. "I'll be right there."

≈

Becca stood frozen to the spot as Luke walked out of her apartment. Her heart seemed to shatter into a million pieces as she watched him leave. She wanted nothing more than to run after him and tell him she loved him, too. Yet she was afraid of the depth of love she felt for him and petrified that something would happen to him, just as it had to Richard. What was she to do?

She made herself clear the table and put on an apron to wash dishes and clean up her kitchen, wishing with all her heart that she could get past the fear of loving again and embrace the life Luke offered her. He'd looked so. . .hurt and alone when he left. Now all she could think was that she didn't want him to think she didn't care.

Becca dried her hands and took off her apron. She had to tell him. But it was getting late, and it wouldn't look right to be knocking on his door at this hour. Instead, she placed a call through the operator, but he didn't answer. At first Becca thought it was because he thought it was her. But then she reminded herself that Luke ran this building and worked for Marcus. He would answer his telephone.

She hung up her earpiece and sighed. Perhaps he'd gone for a walk. Men could do that this time of night. There was nothing to do but wait until tomorrow. She could only pray that it wouldn't be too late and that he would still care.

fifteen

The next few days were some of the longest Becca had ever spent. She'd awoken the day after Luke told her he loved her only to find a note slipped under her door telling her that he had been called off on an assignment for Marcus and that he wanted to talk to her when he got back.

She had problems concentrating at school all that day, and her students asked her if she was all right. The weekend was no better. Saturday loomed long and lonely, and not even her lunch with Natalie and Abigail helped. Natalie had decided to go back to Eureka Springs to decide if she really wanted to move or stay there and see what happened with her and the new minister.

"I'm just having a hard time knowing what to do." She chuckled and shook her head. "I know I am very spoiled. I always have been." She looked at her aunt. "And you've done your share."

Abigail smiled and nodded. "I have."

"I know that it's time I grow up and make a decision about what I want to do with my life," Natalie said with a sigh. "But then I think that there might be a chance for true love for me back home, and I feel I must see what transpires, if it is possible that I could be a good minister's wife."

"Well, you know I am going to miss you greatly," Abigail said. "But it is your life, and I just want you to be happy no matter where you are. Come back and visit as often as you can."

"I will certainly do that. But I have to admit that I do miss Papa and Mama and Lydia and Eleanor. And I am hoping that Becca will come home for a month or two this summer."

Becca had thought she might go home to visit for a week or two, but now that things were so unsettled between Luke and her, staying here for most of the summer might not be an option. But she'd be back. She'd come to love Hot Springs and her students. She might have to find another place to live if things got too uncomfortable. She hoped that didn't happen, but there was no way of knowing until Luke returned. Still, she wasn't going to commit to any certain length of time with her family right now.

"I wasn't thinking of that long a visit right now," Becca said. "But school isn't out yet, so you never know."

"Well, since I'm leaving next week, why don't we spend the rest of the day together? We could go to that new moving picture show that is in town."

"That sounds good. Then you could come back and have dinner with me after the movie. You could stay over, and we could go to church together tomorrow."

"I'd like to stay over," Natalie said. "But don't think for a minute that I'm going to let up on getting you to come back home for longer than a couple of weeks."

Abigail and Becca looked at each other and laughed. Abigail shook her head. They both knew just how persistent Natalie could be.

Abigail decided against going to the movie, but she offered for her and Marcus to pick Becca and Natalie up the next morning for church.

"That would be nice, thank you," Becca said.

"It seems the least we can do since Marcus sent your escort out of town," Abigail said.

Becca didn't quite know what to say. It was possible that Luke wouldn't want to escort her anymore—not after last night. She was thankful that Natalie filled the silence.

"We'll be over to collect my overnight bag when we get out of the movies, Aunt Abby," Natalie said as they got ready to go their separate ways on the boardwalk outside.

"Why don't you both have dinner with us? That way you won't have to prepare anything when you get home. In fact, why don't you collect Becca's things and stay overnight with us? That would be so nice."

Becca had a feeling Abby was more upset than she let on about Natalie's going back home. She probably wanted to spend as much time with Natalie as she could before her niece left. As for herself, it would be a wonderful distraction that would keep her from listening for every footstep down the hall and wondering if Luke might be home. She smiled at Abigail. "That would be very nice. Thank you. We'll pick up my things and come over after the movie, then."

Abigail hugged them both before she left, and she whispered to Becca, "Thank you, sweet friend. I know you understand. Just don't you decide to leave, too."

She waved to them both and went in one direction while they took off in the other.

❧

By Monday, Becca was even more thankful than usual that she had Natalie and the Wellingtons in her life. Staying with them through the weekend helped keep her busy, but it couldn't keep thoughts of Luke out of her mind. He was always there, waiting to fill any moment of silence.

Tonight, as she made her supper, her thoughts flitted from the first time they met to every moment they'd spent together since. Cooking together, going to church, and spending Sunday afternoons at the Wellingtons' and going for rides. Having supper at one of the hotels. His kisses. She remembered everything up to and including the night before he left and his declaration of love quickly followed by his insistence that he wasn't right for her. She didn't think she'd ever forget the expression on his face when he left that night. Now she just wanted him home so that she could tell him she loved him, too—enough so that she would accept that he felt he must continue to work as a Wellington agent and would leave his safety in the Lord's hands.

She had to tell him how she felt. He was a wonderful man who loved the Lord and tried to live his life in a way that gave glory to God. He was kind to everyone. She couldn't remember him being rude to anyone at any time. And he loved her.

Her heart swelled just thinking about the honor of having him love her. Yes, it was natural that she might fear for his life after what happened to Richard, but she'd come to the conclusion that she'd have to deal with it. And with the Lord's help, she would. Luke was her very best friend, and he was the man she wanted to spend the rest of her life with. She just wanted him home so she could tell him so.

Perhaps he'd be back tomorrow. She straightened up her parlor and emptied her trash into the receptacle outside the kitchen. She moved through the doorway then turned to lock the door, when the man she kept running into suddenly appeared and grabbed the side of the door.

"Good evening, Miss Snow," he said.

Sudden fear gripped her. Becca tried to push the door, but the man was too strong and pushed back. He burst into the kitchen brandishing a gun, and Becca finally knew where she'd seen him. She turned to run, pushing anything in front of her away, trying to trip the man up.

"Stop or I'll shoot!" the man said, dodging a lamp she threw.

"No!" Becca screamed.

❧

Luke's nerves were strung taunt. He'd been waiting for days to get this thug, and he prayed tonight was the night. Things had been put on hold over the weekend when Becca had stayed with the Wellingtons. Marcus hadn't planned on that, and while they were both glad she was safe, it wasn't going to help them get the man when he made his move.

But he was ready, too, of that they were certain. Nelson had followed the man to Eureka Springs and found that he was watching the Snow family home and the school Becca had taught at. When Burrows caught a train back to Hot Springs after his visit to the school, they figured he was ready to make a move. The only thing they didn't know was why he was watching Becca so closely.

Now as Luke stood inside his darkened office and looked outside, waiting for Nelson's signal that Burrows was about to make a move, he prayed silently. *Dear Lord, please keep Becca safe. I know we have men stationed everywhere, but anything can happen. We don't know what this man wants or how dangerous he is, but You do. Please watch over her and let us get to him before he gets to her. I pray this in Jesus' name. Amen.*

He saw the flicker of a match being lit from across the street and knew that Burrows was making his way toward the building. Luke signaled to George to move up the back way while Luke hurried up the main staircase to stand in a darkened alcove where he could see the front door to Becca's apartment. He waited for Burrows to come up the stairs and approach it. And he waited.

But Burrows wasn't coming. What if. . .

Luke remembered that he'd shown the man a floor plan of the building when he'd inquired about an apartment. What if he came up the back way and went to—

"No!"

Luke took off in a run at the sound of Becca's voice. *Dear Lord, please let me be in time.* He kicked the front door and burst in.

❧

The front door flew open, and Luke ran in, pushing Becca into the hall before he tackled the man who'd shot Richard and left him to die in her arms. Men seemed to come from nowhere—two coming in from the kitchen door and two more behind Luke.

Becca prayed with everything she could as she watched Luke wrestle the gun away and hold it on the man while two of the men helped subdue the man who was still trying to fight. One of the other men called the police, and another stood guarding her. Becca assumed they were all agents of the Wellington Agency.

Her heart felt as if it were going to burst right out of her chest as Luke led her back into the apartment and set her down on the couch. "We've had a man tailing him for several weeks, and we finally put it all together," he said. "That's the man, right? The man who robbed the bank and shot your fiancé?"

Becca could only nod and whisper, "Yes. But I didn't remember him until tonight when he burst in the service door with his gun. It all came back to me then." Becca shuddered and began to tremble at the memory. She was still breathing hard when the police showed up. Two of them handcuffed the man and took him out while one stayed behind.

"Miss Snow? I need to ask a few questions, if you are up to it."

"She's pretty shaken, officer. I could bring her down to the station tomorrow if—"

"No, Luke. It's all right. I can talk now," Becca said.

There was a knock on the open front door, and they looked up to see Mrs. Gentry. "Are you all right, dear?"

"I'm fine now, thank you. I just need to answer a few questions."

Mrs. Gentry came inside. "Well, I'll go make you a cup of tea and straighten up a bit while you talk, if that's all right."

"That would be wonderful. Thank you." Becca felt like crying, but she didn't know if it was because of the woman's sweetness, because she'd been so frightened, or because Luke was home and sitting beside her, holding her hand. There wasn't time to think about it as the officer began asking questions. She tried to compose herself.

"Miss Snow, do you know this man we know as Burrows?"

"I don't know his name, but I've run into him several times since I moved here."

"Did you know who he was?"

"No. Not until tonight. He always looked familiar to me, but I couldn't place him until tonight when he burst into the apartment."

The policeman was writing everything she said down on a tablet, and he paused to finish his notes before asking another question. "Who is it you believe him to be?"

"I believe he is the man who robbed a bank in Eureka

Springs around a year and a half ago. He also killed my fiancé, who was a policeman and tried to stop the robbery. Richard died in my arms."

The officer looked at her. "Richard Melton?"

"Yes."

"I remember that well. Richard was my wife's cousin. I'm sorry. I'm sure this is very hard on you."

"Thank you. I'm all right now. Do you have any more questions?"

"I think that does it for now. Obviously he must have been after you because he was afraid you would remember him. He has several other aliases, and I'm sure we'll link him to other robberies before we're through. But he did himself in this time. He'll get what's coming to him—I can assure you of that. We'll need to talk to you later and most likely will need you to be a witness, but I think that's all for now."

"Thank you," Becca said. She was beginning to shake harder, and she knew it was just a delayed reaction to all that had happened that night.

Luke saw the policemen and the other agents out while Mrs. Gentry brought a pot of tea to Becca and poured her a cup. "I'm so glad you are all right. I've noticed that man from across the street several times. If I'd known he was after you, I'd have called the police, my dear."

Becca patted her hand. "There was no way to know. Please don't feel bad. Thank you so much for the tea. It is just what I need." She barely managed to lift the cup and saucer without sloshing tea over the side. After a few sips, she began to feel better.

"I'll be going now, dear. But if you need anything, don't hesitate to let me know."

"Thank you, Mrs. Gentry."

Luke came back just as Mrs. Gentry left, and he stood looking at her for a moment before taking the cup and saucer and putting them on a side table. Then he took her hands in his and pulled her up into his arms. "I was so afraid I wouldn't get here in time. Oh, Becca, I don't know what I would have done had anything happened to you."

"You saved my life, Luke. I don't know what would have happened had you not been here. Most probably I wouldn't be here. I believe he would have killed me if you hadn't come just then."

"I think that was his intention. And while I want to say that you were never in any danger, you were. Part of that was my fault. I forgot I'd shown Burrows a floor plan and didn't realize he might use the service stairs. I should have. I am so sorry he got as close as he did. The plan was to stop him before he could get to you."

"It wasn't your fault. And I'm safe now." Becca had never felt so protected and secure as she did standing in the circle of Luke's arms. "I—Luke, I missed you so. I've found there is no guarantee for anyone to be safe. I can't live my life in fear of what might happen any longer. I love you, too, and I am so sorry that I didn't tell you the night you told me how you felt—I—please forgive me—"

Luke pulled back and looked into her eyes. "Did you say you love me?"

Becca nodded. "I hope you haven't changed your—" She couldn't say any more because Luke cut her off with a kiss that answered her question quite satisfactorily. He still loved her. *Thank You, Lord.*

When she broke off the kiss and looked into his eyes, she

could see how much he cared.

"Becca Snow, I love you more now than ever, and I expect to love you more each day. I will resign from the agency, if you will marry me."

Becca's eyes filled with tears of love and gratitude. Not only had he saved her life and captured that man who took Richard's life, but he was also a very forgiving man. He still loved her, and he wanted to spend the rest of his life with her. He was even willing to change his profession for her. But she couldn't let him do that. "Luke Monroe, I love you with all my heart, and there is no need to resign from the Wellington Agency. I found out all too well tonight that it comes in very handy to have a Wellington agent watching over me. I can't ask you to give it up. And yes, I will marry you and love you for the rest of my life, and I'll trust the Lord to keep you safe."

As Luke's lips claimed hers once more, Becca thanked the Lord above for giving her a love to cherish.

A Letter To Our Readers

Dear Reader:

In order that we might better contribute to your reading enjoyment, we would appreciate your taking a few minutes to respond to the following questions. We welcome your comments and read each form and letter we receive. When completed, please return to the following:

Fiction Editor
Heartsong Presents
PO Box 719
Uhrichsville, Ohio 44683

1. Did you enjoy reading *A Love to Cherish* by Janet Lee Barton?
   ❑ Very much! I would like to see more books by this author!
   ❑ Moderately. I would have enjoyed it more if

   _____

   _____

   _____

2. Are you a member of **Heartsong Presents**? ❑ Yes ❑ No
   If no, where did you purchase this book? _____

   _____

3. How would you rate, on a scale from 1 (poor) to 5 (superior), the cover design? _____

4. On a scale from 1 (poor) to 10 (superior), please rate the following elements.

   ____ Heroine   ____ Plot
   ____ Hero   ____ Inspirational theme
   ____ Setting   ____ Secondary characters

5. These characters were special because? _____

_____

_____

6. How has this book inspired your life? _____

_____

_____

7. What settings would you like to see covered in future
   Heartsong Presents books? _____

_____

_____

8. What are some inspirational themes you would like to see
   treated in future books? _____

_____

_____

9. Would you be interested in reading other **Heartsong
   Presents** titles? ❏ Yes ❏ No

10. Please check your age range:
    ❏ Under 18   ❏ 18-24
    ❏ 25-34   ❏ 35-45
    ❏ 46-55   ❏ Over 55

Name _____

Occupation _____

Address _____

City, State, Zip_____

MOUNTAINEER DREAMS

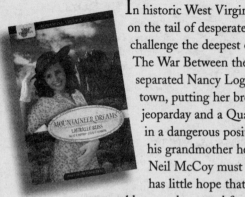

In historic West Virginia, love comes on the tail of desperate times that challenge the deepest of faiths. The War Between the States has separated Nancy Logan's state and town, putting her brother's life in jeoparday and a Quaker doctor in a dangerous position. To give his grandmother her dying wish, Neil McCoy must marry, but he has little hope that a sane woman would respond to an ad for a bride in 1916. The Second World War enters Lucy Bland's backyard when soldiers come to train for rock climbing, led by a particularly handsome captain.

Historical, paperback, 352 pages, 5⅞₁₆" x 8"

Hearts♥ng

Presents

Great Inspirational Romance at a Great Price!

Heartsong Presents books are inspirational romances in contemporary and historical settings, designed to give you an enjoyable, spirit-lifting reading experience. You can choose wonderfully written titles from some of today's best authors like Wanda E. Brunstetter, Mary Connealy, Susan Page Davis, Cathy Marie Hake, Joyce Livingston, and many others.

When ordering quantities less than twelve, above titles are $2.97 each.
Not all titles may be available at time of order.

SEND TO: **Heartsong Presents Readers' Service**
P.O. Box 721, Uhrichsville, Ohio 44683

Please send me the items checked above. I am enclosing $ _____
(please add $4.00 to cover postage per order. OH add 7% tax. WA add 8.5%). Send check or money order, no cash or C.O.D.s, please.

To place a credit card order, call 1-740-922-7280.

NAME _____

ADDRESS _____

CITY/STATE _____ ZIP _____

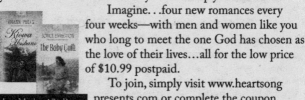